THE ADVENTURES OF

The Junior Jedi Knights

THE GOLDEN GLOBE

Anakin and his new friend Tahiri take a forbidden trip down a river near the Jedi academy. They are drawn by the Force—but for all they know it could be the dark side!

LYRIC'S WORLD

Anakin and Tahiri discover carvings deep within the caves of Yavin 8. These carvings might be able to break the curse of the Golden Globe! But there is something waiting for them in the caves . . .

PROMISES

Before she joined the academy, Tahiri lived with the strange and dangerous Sand People of Tatooine. To learn about her real parents, she and Anakin will have to use the Force like never before . . .

THIS BOOK ALSO CONTAINS A PREVIEW OF THE JUNIOR JEDI KNIGHTS' NEXT EXCITING ADVENTURE: *VADER'S FORTRESS*

Coming in July 1997!

The *Star Wars: Junior Jedi Knights* Series

THE GOLDEN GLOBE

LYRIC'S WORLD

PROMISES

ANAKIN'S QUEST

Rebecca Moesta

BOULEVARD BOOKS, NEW YORK

STAR WARS: JUNIOR JEDI KNIGHTS: ANAKIN'S QUEST

A Boulevard Book / published by arrangement with
Lucasfilm Ltd.

PRINTING HISTORY
Boulevard edition / April 1997

Cover illustration by Eric Lee.

For information address: The Berkley Publishing Group,
200 Madison Avenue, New York, New York 10016.

The Putnam Berkley World Wide Web site address is
http://www.berkley.com/berkley

ISBN: 1-57297-136-3

BOULEVARD
Boulevard Books are published by The Berkley Publishing Group,
200 Madison Avenue, New York, New York 10016.
BOULEVARD and its logo are trademarks
belonging to Berkley Publishing Corporation.

PRINTED IN THE UNITED STATES OF AMERICA

10 9 8 7 6 5 4 3

To Kevin J. Anderson
for showing me that my dreams
were all within reach

ACKNOWLEDGMENTS

Thanks to Lillie E. Mitchell and her flying fingers for transcribing my dictation; Lucy Wilson, Sue Rostoni, and Allan Kausch at Lucasfilm for their help; Ginjer Buchanan at Berkley/Boulevard for her wholehearted support and encouragement; and Jonathan MacGregor Cowan for being my enthusiastic supporter, test reader, and brainstormer, and for being so patient with me while I wrote my first "Solo" novel.

STAR WARS®

Junior Jedi Knights

Anakin's Quest

PROLOGUE

Anakin Solo watched as stars popped into focus in the blackness all around him. Beside him his father, Han Solo, piloted the *Millennium Falcon*.

"Not a bad hyperspace jump, if I do say so myself," Han said with a grin. "You worried about anything?"

Anakin gave the question serious thought. He wasn't sure he knew the answer. "Why?"

"You seemed kinda quiet on your visit at home—more quiet than usual, I mean. Mom wondered if anything was bothering you. Even with all the work she does running the New Republic, your mom notices these things, you know." Anakin's mother, Leia Organa Solo, was the head of the New Republic's government.

Anakin blinked out the viewport at the stars.

They seemed to blink back at him like a million silver-eyed creatures watching him in the night.

"I don't know what's wrong," Anakin said at last. They both fell silent for a while.

"There it is," Han Solo said at last, pointing at the small jungle moon of Yavin 4.

Anakin nodded. He would soon be back on Yavin 4 at the Jedi academy, where his uncle Luke Skywalker trained students to use the Force.

"You know, kid," Han Solo began, "you're still pretty young to be going off to school like this a couple of months at a time. Maybe it wasn't a good idea to start your training so early. Jacen and Jaina were a bit older when they started at the Jedi academy. You don't really have to go back yet. If you wanted, you could stay home for another year or so. Your choice."

Anakin watched the jungle moon grow bigger in the front viewport. He smiled at the mention of his brother and sister. Sometimes he *felt* older than the twins, in spite of the year-and-a-half difference between his age and theirs. He felt as if there was an oldness deep inside his mind. It was something he couldn't explain—not even to himself. He wanted to understand the strange feeling he had, and the strange dreams that visited him each night.

"Thanks, Dad," Anakin said at last. "It's good to know I have a choice. But I want to go back to the Jedi academy. I miss you and Mom when I'm away, but I see Jacen and Jaina almost as much on Yavin 4 as I do at home. Besides, I have my friends Tahiri and Ikrit, and Uncle Luke watches out for me. Don't worry, I'll be fine." But Anakin's words were more sure than he felt.

"Okay, son," Han Solo said. "Back to school it is."

Hours later, Anakin stood beside his uncle Luke Skywalker and the barrel-shaped droid Artoo-Detoo, waving goodbye as the *Millennium Falcon* took off. The blast from the repulsorjets blew their hair around their faces and into their eyes.

Blond hair and brown. Light and dark.

Anakin wondered if the light and darkness meant anything.

As if he understood the direction of Anakin's thoughts, Luke Skywalker put a hand on his nephew's shoulder. "I have to get back to my other students now," he said, "but I think we need to talk. Let me know when you're ready."

Artoo-Detoo beeped once to show that he agreed.

Anakin watched in silence as the Jedi Master walked back to the pyramid-shaped temple that held the Jedi academy. The ancient stone blocks of the Great Temple seemed older than he remembered.

Colder, darker . . .

Anakin shivered. When he figured out what was bothering him, he would talk to his uncle.

He hoped it would be soon.

ONE

Anakin pushed a fringe of dark hair away from his ice blue eyes and looked around. Something felt different here at the Jedi academy. The ancient stone walls of his student quarters still looked the same. After all, he had only been gone three months. The room seemed no different than it had on the day he had left. Everything was in its place: the wooden chest that held his clothes, the small table and chair in the corner near the window slit, the narrow but comfortable sleeping pallet.

The room was not large, but it held everything he needed, and he had always found comfort here. But today it all seemed strange somehow.

Anakin walked to the window and leaned against the thick stone ledge. He looked out to where the lush green jungles crept close to the Jedi academy.

He wondered if Ikrit was somewhere o
now.

Ikrit was a white furry creature wit
whom Anakin and his friend Tahiri had
ing beside a golden globe in a nearby temple ruin. With Ikrit's help, Anakin and Tahiri had discovered the secret necessary to free a group of trapped spirits from the mysterious globe. So far, only Anakin, his uncle Luke, and Tahiri knew that Anakin's "pet" was really a Jedi Master.

Ikrit was not ready to tell everyone who he was, so he had decided not to go home with Anakin for his visit. After their adventures, Ikrit had chosen to stay on Yavin 4. "I have much to consider," the furry Jedi Master had said. "I will stay here and think."

Anakin sighed and shook his head. He felt restless and strange, but the jungle didn't seem to hold the answer to what was bothering him.

Maybe he only felt odd because he was back at the Jedi academy and he hadn't seen his friend Tahiri yet. Tahiri was two years younger than Anakin and had been adopted at the age of three by Sand People on the desert planet Tatooine after her parents were killed in a raid. About a year ago, the Jedi instructor Tionne had met Tahiri, discovered she was strong in the Force, and brought her to study at the Jedi academy.

Anakin sat down on his sleeping pallet, his back against the wall, knees pulled up to his chin. Letting his eyes fall half shut, he reached out with the Force, trying to find the source of his worry. He clasped his hands around his legs and rested his chin on one knee.

Maybe Master Ikrit would be able to sense the cause of his anxiety. Or Uncle Luke.

Maybe . . .

Darkness. Light.

White mist rising against inky black, as it might in a swamp at nighttime.

The air around him crackled with energy.

Maybe his eyes had adjusted, for there was no light, but suddenly he saw the figures. Although they had never met, he knew who they were: Emperor Palpatine, and Darth Vader.

The Emperor's face was wrinkled and marked by the dark powers he loved to use. Shrouded in shadowy robes, the Emperor's face showed a sickly, greenish white. The shriveled lips moved, and Anakin heard a rasping voice say, "Come, my child."

Darth Vader stepped forward and threw a black cloak around Anakin's shoulders. Vader's mechanical breathing echoed in Anakin's ears, but he could not take his eyes off the Emperor.

A story. He had heard a story—or was *it only a story?—about the Emperor. According to the tale, the Emperor's clone had touched Leia's stomach not long before Anakin was born and had claimed the child for the dark side of the Force. . . .*

Now, Darth Vader pressed a lightsaber into Anakin's hand. Vader's cape swirled about him as he lifted something high, high over Anakin, as if to place a crown on his head.

Anakin looked up. A helmet. A dark helmet. Black as a starless night.

Anakin backed away, wordlessly shaking his head. He threw the lightsaber with a clatter to the floor and tore the dark folds of billowing cloth from his shoulders.

"Come, my child," the Emperor rasped again. "You cannot resist your destiny. It will always be inside you."

Anakin opened his mouth and tried to say, "No, I'll never follow you!" but no sound came out.

Vader stretched out his arms. The fallen cloak and lightsaber sprang to his hands, as though they were pets beckoned by their master.

Anakin wanted to run, but his feet would not move.

The Emperor motioned with one finger, and a wave of sleepiness swept over Anakin. "Take what your grandfather has to offer," the raspy voice said. "We have always been a part of you. . . ."

Darth Vader flung the black cape at Anakin, but this time not around his shoulders. The dark cloth covered his head completely.

Anakin grappled with it, trying to fling it aside. It fought back, as if it had a life of its own.

Still struggling, Anakin fell down, down, down into blackness.

"Anakin," a voice said. Not the voice of the Emperor.

A hand grasped his shoulder. Not the hand of Darth Vader.

"Anakin, wake up. It's me!"

Covers were yanked aside and Anakin found himself blinking up at a pair of sparkling green eyes surrounded by a fall of silky pale yellow hair.

"Tahiri!"

"Well, it's not *much* of a greeting for your best friend, but I suppose at least it's something," Tahiri said, pretending to be insulted.

"Oh, uh—hi!" Anakin pushed himself up to a sitting position, feeling a bit sheepish. "What are you doing here?"

"Well, our ship just landed. Tionne and I had been out exploring—you remember, looking for old Jedi records? Well, anyway, we just got back from this strange planet where there were little spiky weeds all over the ground. I even had to wear shoes." She made a terrible face. "You *know* how I hate that. We went into a treasure vault. There was no treasure, but we did find some holo cubes and some written records. Anyway, we brought them back here, and who should come out to meet our ship but Ikrit? He said you needed me right away, so naturally I had to come, and Tionne said . . ."

Anakin felt a warm glow as the girl's words rushed past him. She could be quite a chatterbox and terribly exasperating sometimes, but Tahiri was, without a doubt, his best friend.

". . . and so I told her that I would bring you with me and we could start training again right away.

Well, aren't you going to say anything? Tionne is waiting for us."

Patches of mist still clung to Anakin's mind. "What? Who?"

Tahiri giggled. "*Tionne*. You know—long silver hair, big pearly eyes, Jedi historian? The one who found me on Tatooine?"

"Yes . . . I know who Tionne is," Anakin said, his groggy mind not catching her point.

"Well, she's waiting for us. Ikrit is with her. We're starting lessons again right away."

Anakin let Tahiri grab his hand and drag him off the sleeping pallet. He'd been napping in his clothes. But he made Tahiri wait while he put his shoes on. Then she hurried him out the door.

"Are you feeling okay, Anakin? You don't look too good. I guess that's to be expected, though. After all, Ikrit did say you needed me. Well, I'm here now, and I think everything is going to be just fine. Anyway, remember that treasure vault I was telling you about? It seems that . . ."

Anakin had to admit that he did feel a little bit better as he followed his friend down the passageway, watching her bare feet pad softly on the cool flagstones. As the dream faded, he realized it had served a purpose.

At least now he knew what was wrong.

TWO

A light breeze blew from across the river toward the Jedi academy, carrying with it the cool moistness of early evening. A thick blanket of white mist clung to the riverbank and swirled around Anakin's and Tahiri's knees as they walked.

The mist was so thick, in fact, that it hid nearly all of Master Ikrit except for his head and floppy ears. The white-furred creature waited patiently beside Tionne. Ikrit was obviously as pleased to see Anakin as Anakin was to see the little Jedi Master. He climbed nimbly onto Anakin's shoulder and draped his tail around Anakin's neck.

"I think he's glad to see you," Tionne said in her beautiful musical voice. "We all are." The breeze blew around them and stirred the white vapor so that Tionne's fine silvery hair looked as though it might have been spun from the mist itself.

"So what are we going to learn tonight?" Tahiri asked. She sounded excited. She grinned at Anakin. "I've been begging Tionne for three months to give me more lessons, but she wouldn't. She said I was too young to study all the time and that I needed to take a break." Tahiri snorted. "As if I *wanted* to take a break from studying the Force."

Tionne said nothing. She lit a torch that she had brought with her from the Great Temple and then winked at Anakin as if they shared a secret—that sometimes it was best not to answer Tahiri, that it was enough just to listen. The Jedi instructor's huge mother-of-pearl eyes shimmered in the flickering light of the torch she held.

Tionne closed her eyes halfway and Anakin could sense the Force flowing through her. Then, to his amazement, the ground mist wrapped itself around her, spiraling and climbing upward. The mist wound itself like a vine around her arm and the base of the torch. Finally, the mist circled the tip of the torch in a glowing white halo. As the fire burned away the water vapor, more mist drifted up to join the hazy ring.

Anakin found himself fascinated by this display. It wasn't until Tahiri said, "Wow!" that he realized it was over.

"Now it's your turn," Tionne said. "This may be a bit new and strange to you. It might surprise you how hard it can be. You've practiced lifting objects before, heavy things and light things. But mist is not an object." Ikrit jumped down from Anakin's shoulder and sat near Tionne, swirling the mist with one small paw.

"Mist has no top or bottom," Tionne continued. "There are no sides to hold on to with your mind. It has no real size that you can grasp. Mist is more difficult to move than an object, and much harder to control."

When Anakin saw Tahiri's brows draw together in concentration and her lips press into a firm line, he rolled his eyes up and to one side, as he often did when he was thinking or solving a puzzle. He reached out with the Force, tried to sense the mist. He patted the mist with his mind, pushed it, swished it.

Nothing happened.

He heard a sound of surprise from Tahiri. "Did I do it? Oh. No, it was just the breeze."

"Do not try to hold on to the mist," Tionne cautioned. "It cannot be held. You must use the Force. Trust the Force."

Anakin took a deep breath and relaxed. His eyes fell half shut. He let himself *feel* the mist. Its moisture was in the cool air that touched his cheeks and in each breath that he took. It was all around him. It flowed. He found that his mind could flow with it.

He heard Tahiri's voice beside him whisper, "Oh! Yes, I see," but he was too swept up in the flow of the mist to watch what she was doing. He let his mind flow into a pattern, the first one that came into his head—a small tree. Suddenly, there before him, through his half-open eyes, he could see it: a small, transparent, but perfectly formed tree. Then, beside his tree he saw a misty replica of the Great Temple appear. Tahiri had added her own mist picture next to his.

Amused, Anakin let the mist flow again. This time he decided to form the shape of his father's ship, the *Millennium Falcon*. Within seconds Tahiri made a little X-wing fighter to hover beside the *Falcon*. Then her craft shifted and became a misty lightsaber with a ghostly blade.

Anakin let the *Millennium Falcon* flow and transform into a second phantomlike lightsaber beside Tahiri's. The two energy blades drifted toward each other and crossed. Anakin and Tahiri both made a misty streamer shoot out from the point where the "lightsabers" touched, as if the clash had released a crackle of energy. Mist swirled behind Anakin's blade as Tahiri's pulled back for another strike. But before they could cross their weapons again, Anakin's lightsaber dissolved and he cried out.

He stumbled backward, slipped, and fell into the soft mud of the riverbank—for in the air in front of him, the mist had formed itself into the shriveled face of the Emperor himself, laughing at Anakin!

The bench in his uncle's office felt hard and cold, Anakin thought. The stone walls seemed icy. Even though he was wrapped in a blanket, he shivered.

Artoo-Detoo bumped softly against Anakin's knee and whistled a sad note. The R2 unit was designed to help pilots fly and make repairs in space. Artoo had helped Luke twenty years ago when Luke flew as a fighter pilot against the Empire's giant space station, the Death Star. The little droid became Luke's companion and still stayed with him now that Luke was a Jedi Master.

"Try to drink some soup; then we can talk," Luke Skywalker said, holding out a bowl of steaming liquid and sitting down beside Anakin.

Anakin shut his eyes and shivered again. The steam reminded him of the river mist and of the laughing face of the Emperor. Without opening his eyes, he reached out, took the bowl, and drank the soup. Warmth flowed into him.

Anakin calmed himself with a Jedi exercise that Luke had taught him. "All right," he said at last, "I'm ready, Uncle Luke." When he opened his eyes again, Luke Skywalker sat waiting, listening. "Is it—" Anakin swallowed hard. "Is it true that my mother was touched by the Emperor before I was born?"

Luke Skywalker pursed his lips. A frown creased his forehead. "A clone of the Emperor touched her," he said carefully. "That clone was a copy of the Emperor's body."

Anakin put down his soup bowl and cleared his throat. "Sometimes I wonder if the Emperor didn't find a way to . . . infect me with the dark side of the Force."

Luke Skywalker smiled at this. A kind smile. "What makes you think that?"

"Dreams," Anakin said, pushing dark bangs out of his ice blue eyes. "Dreams that the Emperor and my grandfather are calling me to the dark side of the Force."

"Your grandfather, Anakin Skywalker, was a good man—" Luke began.

"But he became Darth Vader," Anakin broke in.

"Yes, he made that choice for a while. But at the end, and with his dying breath, Anakin Skywalker chose good over evil."

"What if the same thing happens to me? I may be destined to make the same mistakes that he did."

Artoo-Detoo swiveled his domed head and buzzed twice. It sounded to Anakin almost like "uh-uh." In the simple code that Anakin and Artoo had worked out, that meant he did not agree.

"No one can force you to choose the dark side," Luke said.

"But how will I know that I'll make the right choice? How do I know what's inside me?"

"The Force is inside all of us. It flows through every living thing."

"But the Force has a dark side *and* a light side," Anakin insisted. "When did you first learn what was inside of you?"

Luke gave a soft laugh. "My Jedi Master sent me into a cave."

"And you saw what was in you?" Anakin asked hopefully.

"Yes . . ."

"Then I want to go into that cave too," Anakin said. "I want to see what I have in me—whether I'll choose the dark side or the light."

"That cave is on Dagobah," Luke said, sounding surprised.

"Then take me there, Uncle Luke," Anakin said. "I need to know."

Luke frowned. "I'm not sure that cave will tell you anything you can't find out here."

But Anakin was convinced now; he *needed* to go to Dagobah. "I don't think my dreams about turning to the dark side will go away until I go into that cave," he said.

"But I can't take you there," Luke said softly. "I have too many other students, too many other jobs to do for the New Republic."

"Then get me an X-wing," Anakin said. "I'll fly there myself if I have to."

This brought a rich chuckle from Luke. "I don't think you'll need to do that," he said. "I'll give it some thought and we'll see what we can work out. Meanwhile, contact your parents and find out what they have to say." Luke Skywalker stood. "And now, it's getting late. Try to get some sleep," he said. "Old Peckhum will be here early in the morning, and I'd like you and Tahiri to help with unloading the supplies."

Artoo-Detoo made a few encouraging beeps and whistles.

Anakin smiled. "Will you help us unload the ship too, Artoo?"

Artoo beeped once to mean yes.

"Good night," Luke said, placing a hand lightly on Anakin's shoulder. "I wish you a dreamless sleep."

THREE

Morning dawned bright and clear, without a trace of the previous evening's mist. The *Lightning Rod,* a rickety old supply shuttle, was just touching down when Tahiri and Anakin reached the landing field. The two youngest Jedi trainees trotted out to meet the ship.

Tahiri enjoyed feeling the stubbly grass against her bare feet and the wind blowing through her loose blond hair. She could see that Anakin felt better than he had last night, though he still seemed a bit worried. She could tell he was looking forward to unloading the shuttle as much as she was.

It seemed to surprise everyone but Master Skywalker that Tahiri and Anakin always loved to be given a work assignment. It didn't seem at all odd to

Tahiri, though. What could be more interesting and fun than putting their Jedi powers to practical use?

Watching the *Lightning Rod*'s exit ramp lower to the ground, Tahiri giggled. "We'd better hurry and get the supplies unloaded. The ship looks like it could fall apart any minute."

Anakin seemed to give this serious thought. He closed his ice blue eyes for a minute and then looked at Tahiri. "The *Lightning Rod* is a sound ship," he said. "It may look rickety, but old Peckhum keeps it in good repair."

There was a loud thunk from inside the ship. The cargo hatch opened, and with a grinding wheeze another ramp came down.

Tahiri arched an eyebrow at Anakin. "Sure sounds rickety to me."

Anakin understood machines in a way Tahiri found almost spooky. Maybe it was because he had learned how to solve puzzles at an early age—and machines had so many pieces that fit together to make them work, it was almost like a puzzle.

Anakin shrugged. "I can *feel* it. Trust me: this ship could make the Kessel Run right now if she had to."

More clanking sounds came from inside the ship. Probably the pilot shutting down some equipment. *Probably*.

Tahiri chuckled. "Okay, I believe you." She rolled her eyes. "You and your machines."

As if in answer to her call, she heard a series of whistles and beeps coming from behind her.

"Good morning, Artoo," Anakin said. "Glad you could make it."

Tahiri turned to see the little silver, blue, and white droid rolling across the landing field toward them. "Oh, good," she said. "You can keep track of the cargo list while Anakin and I unload." Just then a long-haired man in a rumpled jumpsuit thumped down the cargo ramp.

"Hi, Peckhum," Anakin said.

Artoo-Detoo warbled a hello.

"Good morning, Peckhum," Tahiri added.

"Well, if it isn't young Anakin Solo," the old spacer said, "and my favorite R2 unit in all the galaxy."

Artoo made an embarrassed-sounding bleep at Peckhum's compliment.

"And good morning to you, too, little Tahiri," the pilot said.

"How was your flight? Is the cargo ready to unload?" Tahiri asked. She had grown up with the quiet, mysterious Sand People on Tatooine, and since leaving there, she loved to talk. "Did you bring anything unusual?" she rushed on. "Master Skywalker assigned us to help you in any way we can. We'll stay as long as you need us. Will that be okay?"

Peckhum gave a loud belly laugh, "Yep, that'll do just fine. Why don't we get started with this unloading." Peckhum transferred his cargo list into a datapad for Artoo-Detoo and headed toward the Great Temple to deliver some messages to Luke Skywalker.

For the next two hours Tahiri and Anakin unloaded supplies. Each of them would concentrate on a crate or piece of equipment and, using the Force, raise it twenty or thirty centimeters off the deckplates onto a floating platform called a repulsorsled. Then they steered the floating sleds out the hatch and down the cargo ramp. Outside, Artoo-Detoo recorded the cargo codes and checked the items off the list on his datapad.

As young as she was, Tahiri had strong muscles, but she would never have been able to lift a single one of the cargo crates without using the Force. Even using the Force, the work was hard. Tahiri perspired from the concentration it took to lift the bulky objects onto repulsorsleds and steer them out of the cargo hold.

At one point, Tahiri stepped on a sliver of wood that had broken off from one of the crates. She was so distracted by the sharp sting that she let the box drop back to the floor of the cargo hold. It missed her bare foot by only a centimeter.

Anakin fumbled once, too. He was floating a bundle of cloth so that Artoo-Detoo could record the item on his list when all of a sudden some folds of dark material blew over him, covering his face. Anakin let go of the repulsorsled with a yell of surprise and backed away from it. Tahiri could sense his relief when she offered to float the bundle the rest of the way back to the Jedi academy for him.

Other than those two minor accidents, everything

went smoothly. At last Artoo-Detoo gave a satisfied whistle.

"You mean we're done?" Anakin asked.

Artoo-Detoo bleeped once for yes.

"But there's still one crate left in the cargo hold," Tahiri pointed out. She tugged at a loose strand of her blond hair and gave Artoo an odd look. "Isn't it on the list old Peckhum gave you?"

Artoo beeped twice. No.

Anakin's ice blue eyes met Tahiri's. "I've got a strange feeling about this," he said. The three of them trooped back up the ramp into the cargo hold, and there, sure enough, was one large crate. Anakin closed his eyes for a moment. "Whatever it is, it's not a machine."

Tahiri closed her eyes too and reached out with the Force. "No, it's not!" Her green eyes flew open and went wide with surprise. "Do you think we should wait for old Peckhum?"

But Anakin was already unfastening the clasps on the cargo box. "Give me a hand with this, would you, Artoo?" Anakin said. Artoo reached out a clamp and helped push up on the lid.

Tahiri moved closer to peer inside—and then jumped back in surprise as something sprang out of the box.

FOUR

Anakin's mouth fell open.

Artoo-Detoo gave a trill of alarm.

For once, Tahiri was silent.

Anakin could hardly believe his eyes. A boy had just jumped out of the shipping crate. Anakin guessed the stowaway was in his early teens, but he had a sturdy build and was already a full head taller than Anakin. Shaggy chestnut hair fell to the boy's shoulders. Large amber eyes with a fringe of dark lashes stared back at Anakin from a proud face. Anakin opened his mouth to say something but was too stunned to find the right words.

As usual, Tahiri saved him the trouble. "Hi, what's your name? What planet are you from? I'm Tahiri, and this is my friend Anakin. What are you doing here? Do you always travel in a box?"

"I am Uldir." The boy's voice squeaked when he spoke, as if it couldn't decide whether it was high or low. "I have decided to be a Jedi. Take me to Luke Skywalker."

Anakin frowned. "It doesn't really work like that. I mean, I don't think anyone just *decides* to become a Jedi. But I'll take you to him."

"And if you really plan to become a Jedi," Tahiri added, "you'd better start calling Luke 'Master Skywalker.'"

The shadowy hangar bay beneath the Great Temple was lit by colored flashes from the lightsaber lesson Luke Skywalker was teaching. The glowing swords were powerful Jedi weapons. Anakin hated to barge in on one of his uncle's lessons, but he didn't know what else to do. Uldir had insisted on seeing him right away.

"Excuse me, Master Skywalker," Anakin said, entering the large, echoing chamber. Anakin always used his uncle's formal title when Luke was teaching. The Jedi Master turned off his lightsaber and looked at Anakin. Luke's tall, violet-feathered student stepped back to wait, still holding her own glowing blade.

"I've brought someone who wants to meet you," Anakin said, indicating Uldir. "He came in on the *Lightning Rod* with old Peckhum." Surprise showed on Luke Skywalker's face.

"He's a stowaway," Tahiri supplied helpfully. "His name is Uldir and he wants to be a Jedi."

Luke's eyebrows went up. If anything, he looked even more surprised than before. "Hello, Uldir," Luke said in a soft, serious voice. "It's not an easy thing to become a Jedi. But if you think you can do it, I'll test you later. I need to finish this lesson first, though. I'm sure you're tired and hungry after your journey. Anakin and Tahiri, please show our guest around. After he's had a chance to clean himself up a bit in one of the rooms, make sure he gets something to eat, and then bring him to my office."

"Can we take Artoo-Detoo with us?" Anakin asked.

Luke turned on his lightsaber again. "Sure," he said. "I think I can spare him for a little while longer."

Tahiri loved to talk. One reason Anakin made such a good friend for her, she thought, was that he liked to listen more than he liked to talk—and that was just fine with Tahiri. She told Uldir all about the Jedi academy. Now and then, Anakin added a few words, but Tahiri did most of the talking. As they took Uldir on his first tour through the Great Temple, Artoo-Detoo trundled along behind them.

"This is the turbolift," Tahiri said as the lift doors opened. "We'll take the turbolift to the top level to the Grand Audience Chamber and see that first."

Uldir snorted. "I *know* what a turbolift is. I'm from Coruscant, and every building there has at least one."

Tahiri noticed that Anakin looked very interested in this piece of news. Even though she was stunned by Uldir's rudeness, Tahiri guessed she ought to try to find out more about him. The doors swished shut behind them and the lift zoomed upward.

"I was raised on Tatooine. We don't have many turbolifts there," Tahiri said. "Did you grow up on Coruscant?"

Uldir nodded. "Coruscant and Corellia and a lot of other places—just about anywhere that had a New Republic military base. I've even been to Tatooine. My parents were pilots for the New Republic fleet," he said. "Mostly flying supply shuttles like that old clunker I came in on."

The turbolift doors opened and they all stepped out into a huge room with a high ceiling and tan stone walls worn smooth by time. The auditorium was full of stone benches and had a raised platform like a stage at one end.

"Are your parents dead, then?" Anakin asked in a low voice.

Uldir flinched. "No, but they might as well be." His voice was full of anger and cracked as he spoke. "I hardly ever see them. They never stay on one planet for more than a few days at a time."

Artoo-Detoo gave a sad-sounding warble that echoed through the huge chamber.

Tahiri said, "My parents were killed when I was three. I never really knew them. I was raised by Sand People on Tatooine. They wanted me to stay with them, but Tionne found me and now I'm training to be a Jedi. Did you learn to pilot a ship?"

"Yes," Uldir said. "My parents want me to be a

shuttle pilot just like them—the most boring job in the galaxy! But I want a job with adventure and excitement. That's why I've decided to become a Jedi."

As the tour went on, Tahiri got Uldir to talk more and more. She and Uldir talked about life on Tatooine. Anakin and Uldir discussed life on Coruscant, the capital world of the New Republic. All three talked about droids and which ones were their favorites. Because Uldir had trained to be a pilot, he liked R2 units, and Artoo-Detoo seemed to approve of that.

By the time Tahiri and Anakin showed Uldir to his room, all of them were friends, and all of them were hungry.

FIVE

Tahiri giggled at Anakin's expression of surprise. They were at midday meal in the main dining hall at the Jedi academy, and Anakin was watching Uldir eat with absolute astonishment. Even Tahiri had to admit that she'd never seen any humanoid—even a teenager—gulp down so much food in so little time.

A cacophony of sounds filled the dining hall. Plates and cups clattered. Students talked, sang, woofed, trilled, and croaked. Liquid sloshed in pitchers. The air smelled of baking pastry, fresh fruit, savory vegetables, and roasted meat.

Tahiri was enjoying herself immensely. She and Anakin had long since finished their own meals, but she could still sense strong hunger and thirst in Uldir, as clearly as if he were talking to her through a comm speaker. Anakin must have sensed it too, because he offered a basket of fresh-baked bread to the stowaway, who was on his third helping of stew. The teen ripped off a chunk of the bread, dunked it in his stew, and took a huge bite. Uldir's words of thanks, spoken around the large mouthful of food, came out sounding something like "fank oo."

Tahiri could remember very well what it was like to be hungry and thirsty. She had lived for nine years on the desert planet Tatooine, where it had seemed there was never quite enough to eat and *especially* not enough to drink. But on Yavin 4 there was always enough. That was one of the things she loved about the academy. Tahiri picked up a wooden pitcher and refilled Uldir's mug with juice. She chuckled when a split second later he grabbed for the mug and drank it dry with noisy enthusiasm.

"Maybe you ought to slow down a bit," Anakin suggested with a look of concern.

"Maybe he's right," Tahiri said. "There's always plenty of good food here." She pointed to a stone ledge near the wall where a birdlike alien was sharing a meal with a Jedi trainee who looked vaguely like a short lizard that stood on two legs. "As you can see, we get trainees here from every part of the galaxy, and the cooks make sure that everyone has the kind of food they need. So why don't you stop eating for now and save some room for evening meal—it's only a few hours away. Besides," Tahiri went on, "it's almost time for us to take you to Master Skywalker. Don't you feel nervous about being tested? Aren't you going to say anything?"

Uldir shook back his shaggy chestnut hair. "I'm not really worried. I've taken my share of tests. Anyway, I'm going to be a Jedi. No test can change that." Uldir filled his mug again, drank some more juice, and shot a grin at Anakin. "Does Tahiri *always* talk this much?"

"No," Anakin said after thinking about it for a moment. "She usually talks a lot more."

Uldir broke into surprised laughter. Tahiri did her best to look insulted, but failed miserably and finally burst into giggles herself.

Anakin smiled too, but when he spoke his voice was serious. "You know, Uldir, becoming a Jedi isn't as easy as you might think."

Uldir shrugged his broad shoulders. "I'm not afraid of hard work."

Tahiri could see the worried look in Anakin's eyes that meant he was thinking about the dark side again. "Sometimes I'm not even so sure *I* should be a Jedi," Anakin admitted, and this seemed to surprise Uldir. "Just *wanting* to become a Jedi can be so . . . dangerous."

"Dangerous—is that all?" Uldir's face cleared. "Don't forget, both of my parents are pilots. They started training me to fly almost before I could walk, so I'm used to danger." He stood up. "Take me to Master Skywalker. I'm ready for anything."

"Okay," Tahiri said with a smile. She pointed to his upper lip. "But I'd get rid of that juice mustache first."

• • •

"We'll wait out here in the corridor," Tahiri said. She and Anakin and Uldir were standing at the doorway to Master Skywalker's study.

"Why?" Uldir said. "Come on in with me. This shouldn't take long."

"Um, are you sure you want us watching?" Anakin asked.

"Won't bother me a bit," Uldir said. His voice changed with a squeak in mid-sentence. He cleared his throat. "Besides, it's always good to have a friendly face around. For moral support, you know?"

"All right, if you're sure you don't mind," Tahiri said.

"Nah." Uldir turned and raised his fist to knock on the arched wooden door. But before he could, it was opened by Master Skywalker. He wore a plain brown robe with his lightsaber clipped to the belt.

"Come in," Luke Skywalker said. If he was surprised that Tahiri and Anakin entered with Uldir, he gave no sign.

Tahiri and Anakin sat against the stone wall on a bench near the door. They wanted to stay as much out of the way as possible so they wouldn't disturb Uldir's concentration for this important test. Artoo-Detoo trundled over to join the two junior Jedi trainees.

Tahiri noticed that Ikrit sat on the windowsill, watching silently. His gaze met hers for a long moment. In his blue-green eyes she saw a deep, ancient intelligence—and great curiosity.

Master Skywalker stood facing Uldir, about two meters away. "So you would like to become a Jedi," Luke Skywalker said.

Uldir looked confident. "Yes, I'm going to be a Jedi."

"Why?" the Jedi Master asked. His voice was almost a whisper.

Uldir's cheeks turned pink and he spread his hands. "I, well, because . . ." He took a deep breath and started again. "Jedi Knights have an important job. Everyone admires them. They uphold justice. They travel through the galaxy and defend the New Republic against all enemies." His amber eyes sparkled with enthusiasm. "And if they're forced to fight, they use their lightsabers and they call upon the powers of the Force and—"

Luke Skywalker held up one hand as if to say that Uldir had explained enough. With a faint smile he asked, "If being a Jedi is that glamorous, why shouldn't everyone become one?"

Uldir put his hands on his hips. "They don't have what it takes," he said. "No guts, I guess. No guts, no glory."

"And you have what it takes?" Luke Skywalker asked.

The sturdy teen threw back his shaggy chestnut hair and squared his shoulders. "Yes, I do."

Luke Skywalker closed his eyes and drew in a calming breath. When he opened his eyes, he spoke in a low voice. Tahiri had often heard the words before. "The Force is an energy that flows from and through all things, binds them together. We can draw an energy from the Force. The more we learn about it, the more we can draw from it. Some living creatures have a great potential for using the Force, others have very little. But even those who have that potential become Jedi only through the proper training and great sacrifice. Will you let me look into your mind to see how strong the Force is there?"

Uldir spread his arms. "Sure, why not? That's what I came for." Then he dropped his hands to his sides and waited.

Master Skywalker moved closer to Uldir. He held one hand palm out toward the teen's forehead and closed his eyes. His brows drew together in concentration.

Tahiri didn't know how long the Jedi Master stood still like that. She lost track of time completely. She closed her eyes and could feel the Jedi Master's mind reaching out, searching, probing.

"Well?" Uldir finally said in a voice that cracked with impatience.

Tahiri opened her eyes to find Luke Skywalker looking sadly into Uldir's face. On the windowsill, Ikrit's front paws were folded against his chest, and his ears and tail drooped.

"The Force is with you," Luke Skywalker said to Uldir, "as it is in all living things." He shook his head slowly. "But I did not find the Force strongly in your mind. There was no answering push against the Force in me. Even our weakest Jedi trainees have that answering strength in their minds." Luke shook his head. "I'm sorry," he said. "I don't see in you the potential to become a Jedi."

Uldir's face flushed bright red. He clenched and unclenched his hands at his sides. "I *will* become a Jedi," he said.

Luke's face clouded and he glanced for a moment toward Ikrit. Tahiri wondered if he was looking to the other Jedi Master for advice on this unusual situation.

"It's possible," Luke admitted. "I've never heard of it happening, though. And there's no way the Jedi academy can let in everyone who wants to study just on the chance that they *might* become a Jedi. You have so much to learn about the Force."

"Then I'll learn," Uldir said. He gritted his teeth and his eyes narrowed with determination. "Give me a chance."

"What about your parents?" Luke asked. "Would they be willing for you to stay here?"

"My parents are dead," Uldir said quickly.

Luke fixed him with a stern look and frowned ever so slightly. "If you want to stay at the Jedi academy, don't ever lie to me," he said in a soft voice.

Uldir's shoulders slumped for the first time. "My parents don't know I'm here," he said. "I don't think they even care."

Luke didn't react. In fact, to Tahiri's surprise, he seemed to relent. "We'll have to find out," Luke said. "All right, Uldir. If your parents agree, I'll let you study for a while at the Jedi academy. But everyone here has a job to do. We all have assignments:

teaching, taking classes, unloading cargo, cooking. If you're willing to put in an honest day's work, you may stay at the academy and attend lectures and classes and learn about the Force. If by the end of three months you have learned enough about the Force to lift a pebble or light a flame, then I will accept you as a full-time student—if you still want to be one."

"I *will* want to—and then I'll become a Jedi. You'll see," Uldir said.

"First we must make sure your parents don't object," Luke answered. "Come with me."

In the Jedi academy's communications center, Tahiri watched Uldir shift nervously from foot to foot. He stood beside Luke Skywalker in front of the large viewscreen, waiting for the transmission from his parents to come through.

Before long, the screen lit with the images of two worried faces. Tahiri admired the way Master Skywalker answered the frantic questions of Uldir's parents, letting them know that their son was all right. Once he had explained where Uldir was and that he was unharmed, Luke Skywalker said, "Your son has a question to ask you," and stepped aside.

Uldir's jaw had a stubborn set to it, and he didn't look up directly at his parents' eyes. "Luke, um, Master Skywalker is going to let me work and study here at the Jedi academy," Uldir mumbled. "But he says I need *your* permission first," he ended grumpily.

His father blew out a puff of breath and looked

relieved. His mother's face lit with delight. "You mean that Master Skywalker will really let you stay?" she asked.

"That's fine with me," his father said gruffly. "We were afraid you'd gone off and joined some pirates," he admitted. His kind amber eyes searched for Luke Skywalker, who stepped back on screen. "I hope you know how to handle him better than we do, Master Skywalker. He's a wild one."

Uldir's mother clasped her hands below her chin, as if pleading with Luke. "He's a good boy, really. He just isn't much interested in our work, and we're not sure *what* to do with him. He always seems to want something more, something different. Do you think you can help him?"

Luke Skywalker put a hand on Uldir's shoulder. "That will be mostly up to your son."

Uldir's mother said, "Thank you, Master Skywalker."

His father added, "And may the Force be with you."

SIX

Anakin Solo stood on top of the Great Temple, panting from his climb up the outer stairway. The late-afternoon breeze dried the sweat that trickled down his forehead. From this high above the ground there was a wonderful view of the surrounding jungle and the river not far away.

But Anakin had not come for the view. He had come to be alone. To think—or maybe to brood.

There was no railing around the platform on top of the pyramid, but Anakin was not afraid of falling. He knew how to use his Jedi powers to keep his balance. He sat at the edge of the stone platform and removed his shoes, in the hope that going barefoot would give him at least a little of the positive bubbliness that Tahiri always seemed to have. He waited a minute to see if he would feel any different. . . . Well, at least his feet felt better.

Far below, Anakin saw tiny figures walking out onto the landing field. It was his uncle and a few of the advanced students at the Jedi academy. Anakin couldn't help watching with interest as a lightsaber flared brightly in Luke's hands. One by one each of the students also turned on their lightsabers.

Lightsabers.

In his dream Darth Vader had tried to give Anakin a lightsaber. He shuddered. The dreams . . . *that* was what he had come here to think about.

On the landing pad the Jedi Master and his students began drilling with their lightsabers. Anakin could hear distant sizzles each time a pair of the energy blades clashed together.

"This I cannot teach you."

Anakin jumped. "Ikrit, you scared me."

"Mmmmm." Ikrit's voice was somewhere between a purr and a growl. "My approach was not quiet, but your mind was on other things."

Anakin looked down at the furry white creature who now sat beside him. He felt silly. "I guess I should have noticed you. I mean, normally I would have. It's just that I'm not really *myself* right now." There was a long pause.

Finally Ikrit asked, "Who are you, then?"

Anakin could sense that Ikrit wasn't making a joke. It was an honest question. Anakin searched in his mind for an honest answer. He sighed. "That's just it: I don't know. I always thought I did. I mean,

I'm a kid whose father just happens to be one of the hottest pilots in the galaxy, whose mother is the leader of the New Republic, whose twin brother and sister just happen to have more Jedi potential than anyone else at the academy under the age of sixteen, and whose uncle also happens to be the most powerful Jedi Master alive." Anakin grinned at his own words. "You know—I'm just an average kid." Below, lightsabers continued to hum and buzz, drawing bright arcs in the air.

"And now?" the furry Jedi Master prompted.

Anakin groaned. "Now I'm beginning to wonder. I've been having dreams about the dark side. I want to become a good Jedi and use the powers of the light side, but in my dreams, the Emperor and Darth Vader have claimed me for the dark side. What if it's true? What if I can't escape it?"

Ikrit's voice was thoughtful. "*What if* is a question we all must face. How do you propose to answer it?"

"I think if I could only go to Dagobah—" Anakin began.

"Dagobah?" Ikrit interrupted. "That is a small planet, and far away. Why go there?"

"Because that's where Yoda trained Uncle Luke, and he gave him a test, and—"

Ikrit's floppy ears perked up and he looked more interested than ever. "Please tell me," he said, "about Luke and Yoda and Dagobah and the test. . . ."

Planetshine from the orange gas giant of Yavin streamed in through the narrow window slit of

Master Luke Skywalker's chambers at the Jedi academy. The night air was still warm and Luke had pulled aside the heavy curtains to let in the soft breeze and the spicy scent of jungle flowers. Although he had been lying down for at least an hour, sleep would not come. He relaxed and let himself enjoy the beauty of the soft light.

Somehow, when the furry white form of Jedi Master Ikrit appeared on his windowsill, Luke was not surprised. "Welcome," Luke said, sitting up slowly and motioning for Ikrit to come in. "What brings you here tonight?"

"Concern for the boy," Ikrit said.

Luke nodded. He knew that in some strange way the alien Jedi Master felt drawn to watch over and protect Anakin.

"He seems to think," Ikrit went on, "that only a journey to Dagobah can show him what he truly is inside."

"I sometimes wonder," Luke said softly, "if Leia was wrong to name Anakin after his grandfather, a Jedi who fell to the dark side."

"In the end," Ikrit pointed out, "you turned him back to the light side."

"In the *end* . . . ," Luke agreed.

"The boy is strong in the Force," Ikrit said. "Stronger perhaps than he knows."

Luke nodded. "And when he's with his friend Tahiri, he's even stronger."

"A strong Jedi will he be," Ikrit said, "with the chance to do great good, or—as the boy fears—great evil. The boy will not feel free to finish his Jedi training until he has made this journey and looked inside himself."

Luke realized that the alien Jedi Master was right. "Anakin needs more time and training than I have to give him," Luke admitted. "When Yoda taught me, he had no other students, but I have so many to train it could be months before I can break free to take Anakin to Dagobah." Luke thought for a moment. "I might be able to send Tionne with him. She could leave sooner than I could." He sighed. "But I'm not certain she can help Anakin face this test. She's a wise Jedi, but she has never come face-to-face with the dark side in the same way I have . . . and as Anakin has."

"I will take the boy to Dagobah myself, if you will permit it," Ikrit said.

Luke looked at the white-furred Jedi in surprise. Why hadn't the thought occurred to him? Luke knew so little about this alien Jedi Master. He could sense the goodness in Ikrit and that Ikrit would do anything to protect Anakin. Luke chuckled as a thought struck him. "I don't think Tahiri will agree to let Anakin out of her sight."

Ikrit made an odd wheezing sound and Luke guessed that this was the Jedi's way of laughing. "No, you are right," Ikrit said. "I will take the girl as well."

Luke wondered if this could be the solution he had been looking for after all. Anakin needed time and attention from a Jedi Master, and here was a Jedi

Master offering just that. Luke began to think practically. "How would you get to Dagobah? Can you pilot a ship?"

Ikrit's large fluffy ears drooped in the moonlight. "I have been a pilot, yes. But I was asleep for hundreds of years before the children wakened me. I am not familiar with your newer ships." The ears pricked up again. "The supply shuttle is still here—would the pilot take us to Dagobah?"

Luke was doubtful. "Old Peckhum fly you in the *Lightning Rod*? It's a pretty long hyperspace jump to Dagobah. I'm not sure his ship could make it."

"The boy claims that the ship is much more sound than it looks," Ikrit replied. "After all, one should not judge a ship based solely on the looks of its hull, just as one cannot judge a Jedi by his appearance." Ikrit swept a paw down his furry form to indicate that he was an unlikely-looking Jedi Master. "Size matters not," he added.

This brought a surprised laugh from Luke. "That's what my old Jedi Master used to say." Somehow hearing Yoda's words from the mouth of the tiny white-furred Jedi helped Luke to make his decision. "All right," he said, "I'll talk to old Peckhum about taking you to Dagobah in his shuttle. I'd feel more comfortable if you had a backup mechanic in the *Lightning Rod,* though. You should only be gone for a week or two at the most, so I'll send Artoo-Detoo with you. If you run into any emergencies he can help Peckhum make repairs."

Ikrit gave a satisfied-sounding grunt. "It is agreed, then."

"I still have to persuade Peckhum to take you," Luke warned.

"If it will help," Ikrit said, "you may explain to him that I am a Jedi Master. I will watch over the children."

"I think that will help," Luke agreed. "After that, there are only two people left to convince."

"Tahiri will agree," Ikrit said. "And Tionne will not object."

"True," Luke said. "But the two people I was thinking of are Anakin's parents, Han and Leia."

Anakin stood with Tahiri and Artoo-Detoo in front of the large screen in the Jedi academy's communications center. On the screen, his mother's face registered alarm.

"Old Peckhum is taking you to Dagobah in the *Lightning Rod*?" Leia Organa Solo asked.

The image of Han Solo put an arm around his wife. "Hey, the *Lightning Rod* may look like a hunk of junk," he said, "but I just helped old Peckhum and his friend Zekk install a new hyperdrive motivator last week. Mechanically, the ship's in pretty good shape."

"And Master Skywalker is sending Artoo-Detoo with us just in case there are any problems," Tahiri piped up.

The little droid warbled and bleeped encouragingly.

Leia looked slightly relieved—but only slightly. She bit her lower lip, her face creased with motherly concern. "Are you sure this will help you get past all of those things that have been bothering you? And are you certain this . . . this quest of yours is the only way?"

"I'm sure," Anakin said. "But I won't stay a minute longer than I have to."

On screen, Han and Leia exchanged a look. "Then you have our permission, kid," Han said. Anakin could tell that it was hard for his parents to let him go on this trip.

"Thanks for understanding, Mom and Dad," Anakin said.

His father forced a lopsided grin onto his face. "Dagobah's a strange planet, you know—you kids keep a close eye on each other."

"We will," Tahiri agreed.

"And trust the Force," Leia added.

SEVEN

Stars, millions of them, stretched into starlines around the *Lightning Rod* as it jumped into hyperspace. Anakin finally let himself begin to relax. They were really under way. They were really going to Dagobah. One way or another, he would soon face his worst fears and find the answer to the question that had been burning in his mind: was he truly doomed to fall to the dark side as his grandfather had, or was there hope that he could rise above the darkness, as Luke had?

Tahiri sat next to Anakin in the cramped cockpit of the *Lightning Rod.* There were only two passenger seats, so Ikrit rode on Anakin's shoulder. Peckhum had rigged a tiny harness of crash webbing for Ikrit that attached to the headrest of Anakin's seat. From this perch, Ikrit could see the front viewport over the head of old Peckhum, who sat in the pilot's seat. Tahiri sat behind Artoo-Detoo, who was clamped down at the copilot's station. Peckhum had removed the copilot's seat to make room for the little barrel-shaped droid.

Tahiri, always the optimist, yanked at a strand of her pale yellow hair and grinned at Anakin. "This is really kind of cozy, isn't it?" she said. "It's a shame we couldn't bring Uldir along. He looked kind of unhappy when we told him we had to go away for a few days. Do you think he'll be all right?"

"He did seem upset at first," Anakin agreed, "but when I got back from packing my bags, he was almost cheerful."

"Well, that's good," Tahiri said, smiling. "He's probably looking forward to the chance to settle in to his new work at the Jedi academy while we're gone."

"He has a lot to get used to," Anakin said. "It'll probably take him some time."

From his place at the copilot's station, Artoo-Detoo beeped once.

"Well, I can tell you," Peckhum said, "it's not always so easy to adjust to changes. It's still hard for me to believe that that furry little pet on your shoulder is really a Jedi."

"A Jedi Master," Anakin corrected.

"If you say so," old Peckhum replied. The long-haired pilot flicked a few switches and double-checked his readouts. "Looks like we're right on course," he said, "so we've got plenty of time to just sit back and get acquainted. What did you say that critter's name was again?"

Artoo-Detoo made a rude-sounding noise, as if scolding Peckhum.

"My name is Ikrit," Ikrit said. "You may talk directly to me now that you know who and what I am."

Old Peckhum glanced back at the furry creature in surprise. It was the first time he had ever heard Ikrit talk. "I guess I'm so used to thinkin' about you as Anakin's pet, I'm not used to thinkin' about you as a person, Master Ikrit."

"Ikrit," the Jedi said. "Just Ikrit will be fine."

Anakin couldn't help smiling. It was pretty funny to watch someone trying to grasp for the first time that Ikrit was a Jedi Master.

"If you'll pardon my sayin' so, Master, uh, er, Ikrit," old Peckhum said, "you just don't look much like a Jedi Master."

Ikrit did not seem offended. "And what does a Jedi Master look like?" he asked.

"Well, um . . . *bigger,* I guess, for starters."

Anakin grinned. "Tahiri and I aren't very big."

"No," Peckhum admitted, "but you're just trainees, and you'll get bigger as you get older. From what I've heard, little Ikrit there is already hundreds of years old."

"This is true," Ikrit said. "Never will I be larger than I am now, and never will my body be stronger than it is now. Many of my people once thought as you do, that I could not become a Jedi Master. Let me tell you a story."

Ikrit rose up on his hind legs and held his paws out before him as if he were drawing pictures in the air with his arms. "I come from a planet called Kushibah in the Outer Rim. My people, the Kushibans, are a simple folk, and my size is normal for our kind.

"The Kushibans from my village are farmers and weavers. They grow silkweed and combine it with the fur we brush from our coats each day and spin it into thread. With the thread we weave cloth and tapestries in every color you can imagine. Our weaving is famous throughout the galaxy."

Peckhum nodded. "Sure. I've seen some of it."

"As a farmer and weaver, my skills were unremarkable," Ikrit went on. "However, when I was still quite young for my kind—a little older than Anakin and Tahiri are now—a Jedi Master came to our planet and visited our village. My people were surprised by his visit, for he was seeking a student to train. I was honored that a Jedi Master should come to our village to search for a student, so I offered to assist him in any way he needed while he stayed on Kushibah. I did not dare present myself to him for testing, but to my surprise, he told me that *I* was the student he had been searching for—just like that!

"I laughed out loud, and so did the people of my village when they heard. 'That's a good idea, Ikrit,' they said. 'Become a Jedi Master. You could always build a lightsaber and use it to help us with the silkweed harvest.' In spite of their joking, I went away with the Master and began training to become a Jedi.

"I had been training only about a year and was still unsure of myself when I went back to visit my family. The people of my village were happy that I came, though they still teased me. The night before the silkweed harvest was to begin, one of our villagers returned from the fields torn and bleeding. She told us that a herd of vicious xinkra—beasts three meters tall who could eat one of my people in a single gulp—were headed down the mountain slopes toward the silkweed fields and the village. One of the monsters had seen her and surged ahead, hoping for a quick meal, but she had outwitted the beast, dazzling its eyes with her harvesting knife so that when it sprang at her it bit down on the sharp blade first instead of her arm. And so she had escaped to warn the rest of the village.

"The Kushibans scrambled through their houses searching for anything to use as weapons. They brought rakes, scythes, hoes, even spindles or bits of cloth, but I knew my people were pitifully armed. They would not be able to defend themselves against the beasts. A few of them brought torches, for fire was the only thing that xinkra truly feared. I knew that if the villagers fought that day many would die.

"I climbed onto a grassy rooftop in the center of the village and spoke to my people. I asked them to trust me, to let me fight the xinkra alone before they attacked the beasts with their weak weapons. And then, without waiting for a reply, I rushed out to the fields to meet the beasts. My people must have trusted me, at least a little, for they waited to see what I would do.

"As the beasts thundered closer, I climbed onto a stack of harvested silkweed. I knew I did not have the strength to fight the xinkra with my hands. A hundred or more of them stampeded toward me, snapping at the air with their sharp fangs and slashing it with their long claws. I knew then that I only needed to change the xinkra's *minds,* so I sent them a picture with my mind. I sent them a picture of the village ahead in flames, red and orange and yellow tongues of fire licking toward the sky. And I sent the picture of food—far away behind them in the forests and streams of the mountains. *Plenty* of food: flying creatures, rodents, reptiles, and fish.

"Within seconds, the xinkra turned and headed back toward their home.

"When I returned to my village, my people greeted me as a hero, for they too had a new picture in their minds. I knew then that I would return to my Jedi Master and become a Jedi Knight, so that I could help to defend the galaxy against the darkness that was rising up to devour it."

"I hope," Anakin said, "that when I leave Dagobah I'll be as sure about being a Jedi as you were when you left Kushibah."

"Well now, little Ikrit, I'm glad you told us that story," old Peckhum chimed in. "Even if you're not very big, seems like you're a mighty fine person to have around when there's trouble."

Uldir huddled in the hold of the *Lightning Rod,* wondering how long it would be until they reached Dagobah. He knew that there was something special about where they were going, that Anakin and Tahiri would be learning something important about becoming Jedi. Well, he had decided, if it was important for them, it was important for him, too—no matter what Master Skywalker thought. Uldir figured it was easier to apologize afterward than to get permission to go along. Besides, he knew he had to take his chances wherever he saw them.

Uldir *did* have what it took to become a Jedi, he was sure. He just needed the right opportunity, the right equipment. And he had to learn the right tricks. He needed to have all the same chances that other Jedi students had, like Anakin and Tahiri. He wondered what his friends were doing up in the cockpit of the *Lightning Rod,* but he couldn't afford to show himself just yet. No, there was still a chance that old Peckhum would turn the ship around if he knew that Uldir was on board.

Uldir smiled as he imagined the surprise on Anakin and Tahiri's faces when he finally showed himself. But for now he would have to bide his time. He was going to be a Jedi. And Jedi had to learn patience.

EIGHT

Tahiri observed the small milky white planet that hung in the front viewport. She looked at Anakin and shrugged. "Looks harmless enough."

"Well, I'm reading millions of life-forms," old Peckhum said, "but no cities, no landing beacons—in fact, no technology at all."

"Sounds like the right world, then," Anakin said.

"Yes . . . ," Ikrit breathed, as if talking to himself. "That would be the right one."

"Are you sure you know how to get us close to the right spot, Artoo?" Anakin asked.

Artoo-Detoo swiveled his domed head around and bleeped once for "yes."

"How does he know where to go?" Tahiri asked, suddenly curious.

"Oh, didn't I tell you?" Anakin said. "Artoo's been here before with Uncle Luke."

"Speaking of your uncle," Peckhum said, "he told me that it might be a bit tricky navigating through the atmosphere and that having Artoo-Detoo along would help. I sure hope he's right—about the droid, I mean. Here we go." With that, the old spacer nudged the nose of the *Lightning Rod* downward so that it pointed straight toward Dagobah.

Before long the ship was surrounded by white mist. Tahiri could see nothing but white through the viewports, no matter which direction she looked. The ship bounced and shuddered a few times on air currents as the atmosphere got thicker.

"Well, this isn't really so bad," Peckhum said, but Tahiri got a funny feeling at the back of her neck when he said it. A feeling that something wasn't quite right. Just then the ship shuddered and jolted and old Peckhum groaned. "All the scopes are dead; I can't get any readings. Look's like we're pickin' up speed, though."

Artoo-Detoo blooped and twittered in alarm.

Tahiri watched as the white mists in the viewports became, if anything, even whiter, and harder to see through.

Artoo-Detoo tweeted a suggestion.

Peckhum looked down at the screen that translated the little droid's words for him. "All right then," the pilot answered, "if you think you can find a good landing spot from here, you go right ahead. I can't see a thing."

Artoo buzzed once in acknowledgment. The *Lightning Rod* hurtled downward through the atmosphere. Tahiri felt her stomach muscles tighten and she gritted her teeth and balled her hands into fists. From her perch on Anakin's shoulder, Ikrit reached out a forepaw to touch her arm.

"It'll be fine," Anakin said. "I've just got a feeling about this."

Artoo-Detoo whirled and bleeped several times. "He says we're almost there," Peckhum translated.

Tahiri tried to keep her voice steady. "Good—the sooner the better."

Suddenly the *Lightning Rod* broke through the cover of heavy clouds into the grayish-blue air over the swamps of Dagobah. Less than a minute later Artoo-Detoo brought the ship in for a landing in a wide marshy area surrounded by incredibly tall trees. The ship slid as it came to a stop, teetered for a moment, and then tilted sideways into the muddy water.

"I *thought* you said you knew the best area to land," the old spacer grumbled.

Artoo-Detoo swiveled his head and gave a few sharp bleeps. Old Peckhum groaned again and shook his head.

"What did he say?" Tahiri asked.

Peckhum looked at the monitor screen. "He said," the pilot explained, "that this *is* the best place to land."

"Well, we made it," Anakin said. "We're actually here." There was a tingling feeling in the pit of his stomach now that he was so close to his goal. He wanted to find the cave and put an end to all his bad dreams. At least that's what he hoped would happen.

"Are you sure you don't want to come along, Peckhum?" Tahiri asked, tugging at a few strands of her wavy pale yellow hair.

"Nope," the old spacer said. "I'm gonna stay here and check out all the ship's systems and make sure everything's in good working condition. Nearly scared the boots off me when my sensors blinked out like that before we landed."

"Boots!" Anakin said. "That reminds me." He looked down at Tahiri's bare feet. "You might want to put something, um, er . . . *on* before we go out there." He knew how much Tahiri hated wearing shoes, so he tried to say it carefully to avoid upsetting her. He could see right away that he had failed, though.

The blond-haired girl planted both fists on her hips. "Oh no you don't, Anakin Solo. You may be my best friend, but I'm *not* putting on shoes—not even for you."

Ikrit unbuckled his crash harness, scampered over to a storage locker, and removed a small knapsack. Anakin had no idea what the Jedi Master was up to. Ikrit tossed the pack to Tahiri, who caught it easily. "The Jedi Tionne packed this for you," he explained.

Anakin watched Tahiri open the sack and rummage through its contents. There was a small medikit, a glowrod, some emergency food packets, and a pair of buttery-soft leather boots. Tahiri blushed, but Anakin couldn't tell if she was pleased or embarrassed. Ikrit handed Anakin a similar small pack of provisions.

Anakin slung the straps over his shoulders and said, "All right then, let's get moving."

Tahiri shrugged and put her knapsack on as well. "Might as well bring it with me," she grumbled. "But I won't promise to wear the boots."

"Sure," old Peckhum said, "you kids go ahead. I'll trust the Jedi Master and Artoo there to keep an eye on you while you get the lay of the . . . uh . . . swamp."

Ikrit scrambled up onto Artoo-Detoo's domed head. The droid, who seemed not to mind, gave a confident whistle. Peckhum opened the exit hatch and lowered the ramp. Together, Anakin, Tahiri, Ikrit, and Artoo walked, rode, or rolled down the ramp.

The air outside was warm and thick with moisture, but the first thing Anakin really noticed was the smell. A heavy, boggy odor clogged the air: mildew mixed with the scent of blooming flowers and rotting plants and a thousand other smells Anakin couldn't name.

"Do you know which direction Yoda's training area was from here?" Anakin asked. Artoo-Detoo beeped once and led the way. Anakin was a bit surprised that the little droid was able to maneuver so well on the marshy ground.

Ikrit gave a thoughtful rumble deep in his throat. "Mmmmm. There is much energy from the Force. Many creatures are here."

"I can sense them too," Tahiri agreed, waving a hand in front of her face, "but the only ones I can really *see* are these bugs."

She was right, Anakin noticed. There were insects everywhere—billions of them flying in swarms.

Tahiri coughed. "I think—I think I just breathed one in." She flapped her hand again, as if trying to wave away the clouds of insects.

"Stay calm, child," Ikrit said. "The Force is in all creatures, even ones so small. Calm your mind. Direct the creatures away from you with your thoughts."

Still following Artoo-Detoo, Anakin let his eyes fall half shut and *thought* at the swarms of insects that buzzed and hummed about him. He imagined the creatures staying away from him, moving back a bit. To his surprise, although the insects did not go away, they came no closer than about ten centimeters—as if there were a tiny force field surrounding him.

"Hey, it works!" Tahiri said.

Anakin looked over at her and noticed that she had managed to repel the insects, too. He was less worried about the animals he *could* see than the animals he could not, however. Walking through the swamp was eerie. The misty air above let little sunlight through and covered the tops of the trees so that the day was never quite light and never quite dark. Shreds of mist clung to tree trunks and hovered above pools of brackish water. A stream of bubbles made a gurgling sound in one of the murky pools. Anakin wondered whether the bubbles came from a submerged spring or from some air-breathing creature that lurked beneath the surface.

Around them on every side, unseen swamp dwellers croaked, hissed, chirped, trilled, growled, and belched. Anakin felt a prickling at the back of his neck and shivered. He hoped it wasn't too far before they came to the cave.

Ikrit seemed to think that it was time for a lesson, because he began to talk to Anakin and Tahiri. "Since the Force is in all things," he said, "it can teach us much. If one can simply learn to listen to the Force—"

Just then a cry rang out behind them, a cry of pain and terror.

It came from the direction of the *Lightning Rod*.

NINE

Tahiri and Anakin cried out at the same time.

"Peckhum!" Tahiri said.

"No!" Anakin yelled.

The two friends whirled and ran back toward the *Lightning Rod*. Ikrit sprang down from Artoo-Detoo's head and dashed after them. The barrel-shaped droid followed, whistling and beeping his distress.

Tahiri's loose blond hair streamed out behind her as she ran. Her bare feet thudded softly against the muddy ground. She was a fast runner, but Anakin kept up with her. She heard the voice calling for help again.

"Hang on," Anakin yelled back, "we're on our way."

Tahiri felt her heart pounding in terror, but not for herself. She jumped over a rotten log and ducked under a curtain of moss that hung from a tree branch. A part of her mind was thinking how proud she was that Anakin had reacted so quickly to hurry to the aid of a friend.

With her next step, Tahiri felt a sharp pain in her foot. She gasped, but there was no time to stop now, she decided. The *Lightning Rod* was just up ahead. She could see it. Limping ever so slightly, she ran the last few steps into the clearing. She panted for breath as she looked around in dismay. There was no sign of the pilot.

"Peckhum, where are you?" Anakin called, running up beside her.

"Heeelp!" A faint voice drifted toward them from the far side of the *Lightning Rod.*

"This way," Ikrit said, scrambling past them. The Jedi Master's white fur was filthy and matted from running through the mud. Tahiri and Anakin followed him to the far side of the ship, where half of the *Lightning Rod* rested in a shallow pool of scummy water.

Tahiri's mouth gaped open with the shock of what she saw there.

"Uldir!"

Uldir nearly fainted with relief when he saw his friends Anakin and Tahiri round the side of the ship. He had been frozen with fright for what seemed like hours; but maybe it had only been minutes since he had opened a tiny escape hatch in the cargo bay of the *Lightning Rod* and climbed out—only to land in what looked to him like a sea of swamp slime.

Of course, Uldir had realized instantly that he'd

made a dreadful mistake by leaping down from the exit hatch without looking first, but it had been too late to correct his error. He'd turned and tried to slosh toward solid ground, but lost his footing and plunged face-first into the muck.

He'd panicked. Thrashing with his arms and legs, Uldir had managed to get his head back above the swampy water, only to find that his struggles had made him sink deeper into the ooze. He was now up to his armpits in the stinking grayish-green water. To make matters worse (if that were possible), his splashing had attracted the attention of one of the ugliest and, well, *slimiest* creatures he had ever set eyes on.

Uldir froze. The thing, whatever it was, had a long sausage-shaped body—about ten meters long, Uldir guessed. Its melon-round head and its long body were covered with slick greenish-gray fur, the same color as the swamp water. The creature raised its bulbous head high into the air above Uldir, then tilted it from side to side, trying to get a good look at him through its six milk white eyes.

Uldir, still frozen with fright, had hoped that the furry snake monster would decide that he was much too large to eat and simply go away. But no sooner had this hope crossed Uldir's mind than the animal bent over and pushed its round furry face close to Uldir's so that he could see its three enormous flat front teeth. The teeth were nearly as long as Uldir was tall. Uldir tried to take a step backward, but his feet were fixed firmly in the mud. A long strand of algae was stuck between two of the creature's front teeth, and when it opened its mouth enough for him to smell its foul breath, Uldir couldn't help himself—he screamed.

The creature jerked its head back and blinked its six milky eyes at him. Uldir thought he heard an answering yell in the distance. The furry snake thing turned its head around almost in a full circle, as if searching for the source of the noise, then swiveled back toward Uldir again. Its melon head dipped down toward him and it opened its mouth again—and gave out a roaring, stinking belch.

Uldir screamed again and used the only weapon he could find. He threw handfuls of mushy algae directly at the monster's mouth.

The creature coughed and gulped and made a loud rumbling sound deep in its throat, but it did not eat Uldir. So, for what seemed like an eternity, each time the massive head approached him, Uldir threw globs of slimy algae and yelled.

Finally Uldir heard a strange wheezing voice he didn't recognize, saying, "Over here!" Then he saw Anakin and Tahiri rushing to help him.

The sausage animal backed up again to get a look at the new arrivals. Uldir glanced around to locate the source of the strange voice but saw no one except Anakin, Tahiri, and Anakin's furry pet Ikrit.

Tahiri called out Uldir's name in surprise.

"Help me get out of here before this monster eats me!" Uldir called back. Tahiri, who seemed to be limping, looked puzzled.

"Can't you swim over here?" she asked.

"No," Uldir said. The creature's face approached again, and he slung another handful of algae at it. "I'm stuck in the mud." Uldir noticed that Anakin's pet had moved away from the water and figured that it must be afraid of the swamp, or of the slimy-furred sausage monster, or of both.

"Stay calm. We're going to get you out," Anakin said. Tahiri took a step toward Uldir, but Anakin stopped her. "It wouldn't be a good idea for us to go out there even if you were a good swimmer."

Tahiri looked sheepish. "Oh—right. We could get stuck, too, and then we wouldn't be any help to Uldir."

"Anyway," Anakin said, "I'm pretty sure that monster won't hurt him. I think I've got an idea to get rid of it."

"I will assist Anakin," Uldir heard the strange wheezing voice say, but he couldn't see who was speaking.

Tahiri stopped to think for a moment. "Okay, I'll get a stick or a rope or something to help pull him out," she said. "A really long branch ought to work, or maybe a vine. I could probably find a rope in the *Lightning Rod*. If not, I might be able to tie some cables together. I can be quite resourceful, you know."

Uldir sighed. He wished the girl would do less talking and get around to rescuing him.

"Are you *sure* you can take care of the, um, wildlife?" Tahiri asked, looking over her shoulder.

Anakin nodded. "I can handle it."

The blond-haired girl limped off to a stand of trees and Uldir saw Anakin shut his eyes and raise his hand toward the furry snake monster, almost as if he were greeting it. The melon head swung around to look at Anakin, cocking this way and that to get a better view.

Uldir wondered if the younger boy was using some sort of Jedi trick to control the animal's mind. Seeing that the beast was distracted, Uldir tried to wriggle free, but only sank deeper in the mud. The smelly water came up to his chin now.

With his eyes so close to the surface of the pool, Uldir saw something very strange happening. Blobs of floating algae were gathering together to form a larger blob. From across the gray-green pool, more lumps of algae floated toward the growing mass. Soon the algae formed a thick pulpy carpet on the surface of the water, nearly two meters wide. It floated slowly toward the furry snake beast.

"Can you reach out to the creature's mind and persuade it to go away?" Anakin asked. Uldir looked toward him and could see that the boy must have been moving the algae with his mind, with the Force. He wondered who Anakin could be talking to—didn't he *know* Uldir couldn't use the Force like that?

The melon head bent toward the surface of the water and slurped up a huge mouthful of algae. The algae floated farther away from Uldir, and the beast followed, munching contentedly.

While Anakin guided the slimy creature away, Tahiri returned with a length of tough vine. She threw one end to Uldir, but it fell short and began to drift out of reach. The girl shut her bright green eyes and concentrated. Uldir was amazed to see the vine begin to drift back toward him. Soon he was able to reach out and catch the end of it.

Uldir pulled, trying to free his feet from the mud. Tahiri leaned backward to pull, but he could see her face crumple in pain as she pushed down hard with both heels to keep from sliding into the water. Anakin and his furry pet quickly came to her aid, but even together they were unable to pull Uldir free.

Uldir strained with his arms, pulling on the vine as hard as he could. He kicked and wriggled in the warm, putrid water. Just as he was about to give up hope, the little R2 droid appeared again, followed by the long-haired pilot. Old Peckhum looked just as surprised as Anakin and Tahiri had been to see Uldir. Without stopping to ask questions, though, the pilot wrapped his huge hands around the vine and tugged. Once Peckhum put his legs and back into it, adding his strength to the group's efforts, Uldir's feet pulled free.

When his feet came out of the mud, Uldir's entire body skidded across the surface of the filthy water like a turbo-ski. By the time Anakin, Tahiri, and old Peckhum hauled him up out of the pool, every square centimeter of Uldir's body was covered with swamp scum. Algae dangled from his hair and grayish-green water dripped from his ears and nose.

"Thank you," Uldir managed to splutter. He coughed up a whole mouthful of swamp water.

"What are *you* doing here, Uldir?" Tahiri asked. "How did you get to Dagobah, and why did you come? What were you doing in the swamp? What was that thing that was looking at you? Does Master Skywalker know you're here? How did—"

"Well, this day's just been full of surprises," Peckhum finally cut in. "But there'll be time enough for questions later. I think we'd better get a certain young man cleaned up."

The idea of being clean and dry suddenly sounded very good to Uldir.

"And"—the old spacer looked at Tahiri—"then I think we'd better take care of a certain stubborn young lady's foot."

Artoo-Detoo gave a loud beep of agreement.

Uldir looked down at Tahiri and saw that her right foot was bleeding. The blond girl blushed a bright red. "Well, maybe I did learn a bit of a lesson about going barefoot on strange planets," she said.

Her comment interested Uldir. Apparently these Jedi trainees weren't so powerful. If Tahiri knew so much about the Force, why hadn't she been able to protect her feet? Uldir was sure that with a little bit of training even *he* could do better than that. Sure, he had had a close call himself just now, but that had been with a monster, not with a little thorn or a pebble.

"Thank you all for rescuing me," he said with real gratitude. "If you hadn't come along, that monster would have eaten me for sure."

"Mmmm. You were never in any true danger."

There was that strange wheezy voice he had heard earlier, Uldir thought. He looked around to see who had spoken. All he saw was Anakin's pet, Ikrit.

"Your danger came from the swamp itself, not from the creature," Ikrit said.

Uldir's eyes went wide. "It—it talked!"

TEN

In the hold of the *Lightning Rod,* Anakin sipped from a cup of warm broth that old Peckhum had made in the food prep unit. Beside him Uldir sat wrapped in blankets, drinking soup and shivering occasionally, even though it wasn't cold inside. Artoo-Detoo puttered and fussed over the wound on Tahiri's foot, making scolding noises while the longhaired old pilot bandaged it.

"I'm sorry I didn't hear you calling for help sooner," Peckhum said. "I had the antistatic generator running while I checked the circuit paths. I couldn't hear a thing."

"You came right when we needed you," Anakin said.

"Well you can thank your furry little Jedi friend here for that," old Peckhum said, winking at Ikrit, who was once again perched on Artoo's domed head.

"Jedi?" Uldir exploded into laughter. "Okay. I'll admit it's pretty amazing that your pet can talk. But don't try to tell me that *that* overgrown furball is a Jedi!" He pointed at Ikrit, whooping and chuckling until tears filled his amber eyes.

Anakin wasn't sure exactly how he had expected Uldir to react to learning about Ikrit. Surprise? Awe? Maybe even discomfort or distrust . . . but not this. Anakin found himself becoming annoyed. If Uldir truly wanted to become a Jedi, this was no way to talk about Ikrit. He looked straight into the older boy's eyes. "Ikrit isn't a trained pet. He is a Jedi."

Tahiri piped up at this point. "Not only that, but he's a Jedi *Master,* and he's hundreds of years old."

Uldir looked from one to the other. His jaw clenched and his eyes grew hard. "Is this your way of getting back at me for stowing away again? First Master Skywalker tells me I don't have the talent to become a Jedi. Now you two lie to me. Do you really expect me to believe that some flop-eared talking pet is more worthy to be a Jedi than I am? That he's a Jedi *Master*?"

Before Anakin or Tahiri could make an angry reply, Ikrit spoke in a low, quiet voice. "Perhaps we can believe the truth," the furry Jedi Master said, fixing his blue-green eyes on Uldir, "only if truth is what we seek."

Morning mist hung in the air like shreds of white gauze, though how one could tell the difference between morning and evening mist—or even afternoon or night mist—was beyond Anakin. It seemed to him that fog hung in Dagobah's air no matter what time of day it was.

All of the companions had gotten a good night's sleep in the hold of the *Lightning Rod*. Now, though, they left old Peckhum behind to tinker with the ship and ventured into the swamp for what Ikrit said was a very important lesson.

Ikrit rode ahead on Artoo-Detoo. Behind them walked Anakin and Tahiri. Uldir brought up the rear of their little group. In spite of the clouds of buzzing insects, the small odd-looking animals that scuttled across their path, and the strange burbling of the marshy water, all of them seemed to be enjoying themselves—all except Anakin.

Anakin looked around at the swampy landscape with barely concealed impatience. Why had Ikrit taken it into his head to conduct a lesson *now,* of all times? He guessed that it had something to do with Uldir's showing up, but that didn't make him feel any better. After all, wasn't it Anakin's quest that had brought them to Dagobah in the first place? Shouldn't they be concentrating on that instead?

The small Jedi Master rapped on Artoo-Detoo's domed head to signal a halt.

"This will do," Ikrit said. He motioned to his three "trainees," then pointed to the trunk of a fallen tree. "There. Sit." Anakin, Tahiri, and Uldir obediently perched themselves on the log.

"Close your eyes," Ikrit said. "Reach out with all of

your senses. Feel the energy around you. Feel the life."

It was easy for Anakin to feel the energy and the life. In fact, he wasn't sure he had ever been on a planet with so *much* life. In its own way, the primitive-seeming planet of Dagobah was every bit as bustling as his home world of Coruscant, just with different life-forms.

"The energy flows around you and through you," Ikrit said. "It is a part of you and a part of all things, and you are a part of it. Even the killing of one insect can change an entire planet, and a small alteration in yourself can change the whole universe. We are all related in an intricate web, all joined through the Force. Everything you do causes a reaction and affects something else. Through the Force we can sense actions and reactions, and that can help us choose the right thing to do. Now you may open your eyes."

Anakin blinked. That was all? That was the entire lesson?

"We will return to the ship now for supplies, and this afternoon we will go to the cave," Ikrit said. "On our way back I will give each of you a chance to lead. I will not interfere. I will only follow."

Tahiri took the first turn at leading. She had to stop a few times to sense the right direction with the Force, but she didn't make any wrong turns or lead them into any boggy patches. When Anakin's turn came, he could tell that Ikrit was pleased with how well Tahiri had done.

Anakin was tempted to hurry back to the ship so they could get on with his quest to find the mysterious cave where Yoda had tested Luke Skywalker. But he knew that the swamp was far too dangerous a place to hurry. He used a Jedi relaxation exercise to calm himself, as Tionne and Uncle Luke had taught him. *Patience,* he told himself. *A true Jedi must learn patience.* He led them at a slow, steady pace, sensing the way with the Force. At one point he felt a large, hungry creature in the undergrowth and was able to guide the group safely around it. Ikrit said nothing at the end of Anakin's turn, but the warm glow of his blue-green eyes was praise enough for Anakin.

"Okay, I guess it's about time I got you swamp-slugs moving a bit faster," Uldir said, shaking back his shaggy chestnut hair and stepping into the lead. His sense of direction was good, Anakin had to admit, and the companions picked up their pace as they followed him. The sturdy teen seemed full of confidence and never hesitated for a moment.

Still following Uldir, the group had almost reached the clearing where the *Lightning Rod* waited.

But something was wrong.

Anakin didn't understand it, but something happened inside him. A shiver ran up his spine and a strange, queasy chill grew in the pit of his stomach. Tahiri grabbed his arm and he could tell by the look in her wide green eyes that she had the same uneasy feeling.

Then, almost without knowing what they were doing, Anakin and Tahiri dashed forward.

"Uldir, stop!" Anakin said.

"Stay where you are!" Tahiri cried.

Behind them, Artoo-Detoo let out a trill of alarm.

Uldir turned with a scowl as the younger trainees reached him and each grabbed an arm. "What's wrong with you two? We're almost there."

"I don't know what it is," Anakin said. "But don't go that way."

"There's something dangerous ahead," Tahiri added.

Uldir snorted. "Oh, I get it. You don't want me to get the idea that I'm a better leader than the two of you, so you're trying to scare me. I'll admit, you had me going for a minute there, but it won't work." He started up the trail again and tried to shake off Anakin and Tahiri.

"Stop." Ikrit's scratchy voice was not loud, but it held the power to halt even the most stubborn teenager. "Your friends wish only to save your life." The Jedi Master jumped down from his perch on Artoo's head and scrambled to the front of the group.

Uldir turned a sour look on the furry creature, but Ikrit paid no attention. Picking a long, thick stem of marsh reed from the edge of a murky pool, Ikrit prodded the air on the path ahead of Uldir. Without a sound, two large chunks of the reed fell to the ground, as if sliced by an invisible laser.

Uldir took a step backward as Ikrit repeated the demonstration, waving the stem through a different patch of what appeared to be thin air. Again, the reed was mysteriously chopped to bits.

"But what could possibly do—" Uldir began.

"A butcher bug," Ikrit replied before the boy could finish. "It spins a web so sharp and nearly invisible that its prey never see it. They are sliced into pieces—and without a fight, the butcher bug has its next meal. If not for Anakin and Tahiri, you might have been the main course."

Anakin felt sorry for Uldir. The older boy's face had gone as pale as Ikrit's fur, and he looked as if he might become sick.

"Would you lead the rest of the way back, Master Ikrit?" Anakin asked. "I think we'd all like to follow for a while."

ELEVEN

Anakin was glad when he and Tahiri, Ikrit, Artoo-Detoo, and Uldir finally set out to find the cave. An almost unbearable tension had been building inside him as they ate their midday meal and packed small knapsacks of provisions for the trek. He could hardly wait now to finish his quest and find out the things he had come to Dagobah to learn about himself.

Anakin hardly noticed that clouds hung even lower, if possible, than usual over Dagobah's swampy surface, hiding the treetops from view. He didn't care that the clouds were the color of tarnished steel or that they drizzled a fine mist on all of the companions as they walked. They were on their way to the cave. That was all that mattered.

Artoo-Detoo was the only one in their group who had actually been to the cave before, so he led the way. Ikrit once again rode atop the little droid, as if he considered Artoo-Detoo his personal steed. Artoo warbled and beeped occasional comments while he trundled down the path. Anakin noticed that Ikrit's blue-green eyes were closed, though, and that he didn't respond. Perhaps, Anakin mused, Ikrit was too deep in thought.

Tahiri, on the other hand, seemed as cheerful and talkative as ever. She had brushed her golden hair and put on a fresh flightsuit. She was also wearing the soft boots that Tionne had made her. Now she bounced along beside Anakin, talking about the very footwear she had once refused to even consider.

". . . and the soles are very tough, but flexible—and waterproof. They're not at all like those icky hard shoes I had to wear so often on Tatooine. Those were made out of stiff animal hides and rubbed blisters on my feet." Tahiri grinned at Anakin and tucked a strand of hair that had come loose back behind her ear. "But these boots are soft enough that I can still feel what's under my feet. I still won't wear shoes unless I *have* to, but these are probably the best . . ."

Anakin was glad to have Tahiri chattering so gaily beside him. It spared him the need to say anything, and Tahiri didn't seem to mind his silence. She talked to Ikrit occasionally, who didn't answer either, and Artoo-Detoo. Artoo tweeted and warbled in return, though none of them could tell what he was saying. Tahiri even tried to draw Uldir into conversation, but the teen seemed to be sulking.

Their trail wound around through the swamps past the knotted roots of huge trees. The knobby roots were as thick around as Anakin's waist. They arched high in the air from the base of each tree trunk before sinking deep into the marshy ground. Sometimes the companions were forced to duck under gnarled roots that grew across their path.

The next time Tahiri spoke to Uldir, he glared at her for a time, and when he finally spoke, he changed the subject. "What's so special about this cave we're looking for, anyway?"

Anakin sighed and wished that Uldir didn't have such a sour attitude. He certainly didn't seem to have learned much of a lesson from his close encounter with the butcher bug web.

"A Jedi Master named Yoda lived on this planet for the final years of his life. He was Uncle Luke's Jedi Master, and this is where he taught Luke all about being a Jedi."

"So?" Uldir said—rather rudely, in Anakin's opinion.

Anakin was starting to get annoyed at Uldir's attitude, so he paused to let out a long slow breath and tried to keep his patience. "Master Yoda sent Uncle Luke into a special cave as a kind of test. Uncle Luke says that there's nothing much inside the cave, except for what you take in with you."

The weather grew worse, and a light rain began to fall. Artoo-Detoo whooped in alarm as his wheels sank into soft mud. Anakin and Tahiri pulled Artoo-Detoo free and Artoo adjusted his motivators and the height of his treads so that he could move better across the soft ground of the trail. Then they all started walking again, their feet making muffled squelching noises on the muddy path.

"The way Uncle Luke explained it," Anakin went on, his eyes rolling up and to the side, "the cave works kind of like a mirror, to show you what's inside your own mind. He said he learned some really important things about himself that day."

Uldir snorted. "You mean you needed to come halfway across the galaxy and go into a *cave* to figure out what's in your head?"

Tahiri stamped her foot in the middle of the trail and rounded on Uldir. Her green eyes were as stormy as the sky above. "This is very important to Anakin. It's his quest. I'm here because I'm his friend. I'm trying to *help* him find the answers he's looking for." Although Tahiri was quite a bit shorter than the stocky older boy, she raised a warning finger at him. "And if you're really Anakin's friend too, I suggest you start acting like one." As she spoke her final words, distant thunder boomed through the air and fat, warm droplets pounded down, completely soaking them all.

Uldir looked stunned for a moment, as if he believed that Tahiri might have called down the thunder and the sudden drenching rain. But then he simply shrugged and said, "Okay. I'm sorry."

At that point Ikrit, who had been roused by the rain, said, "We must take shelter." The Jedi Master waved one furry white paw toward a cavernous opening beneath the gnarled roots of a massive tree.

Artoo-Detoo bleeped once and rolled with Ikrit into the shelter. Anakin, Tahiri, and Uldir ducked in after them. Anakin turned to look out at the pouring rain and was struck by how much the high knobby roots reminded him of the spindly, jointed legs of some enormous spider.

Anakin wasn't really cold, but he shivered anyway. . . .

To his surprise, Ikrit picked up a dry piece of broken root. The Jedi Master closed his eyes briefly, and flames sprouted from one end of the wood, making a torch. Ikrit handed it to Anakin. Anakin knew he could have used a glowrod to light the little "cave," but somehow the torch made him feel more cheery.

Half an hour later the rain began to let up. When Anakin suggested that they leave, though, Ikrit's floppy ears stood straight up and he shook his head. "Not yet—danger lurks somewhere close by."

"I feel it too," Tahiri said. "But what is it?"

Four pairs of eyes and one blinking optical sensor peered out into the gray afternoon. Before long, a very strange-looking creature plodded slowly into view.

Uldir snickered. "*That* thing? We're in danger from that?"

The huge slothlike animal had greenish-brown fur and a wide, soft mouth. It certainly didn't look dangerous, Anakin agreed silently. In fact, he sensed that this was not the source of their danger at all. The beast lumbered over to a cluster of brightly colored mushrooms that grew near the base of the tree. Each fungus in the clump was at least as high as Anakin's waist, and the beast seemed drawn to the mushrooms. It reared up on its hind legs to display a hairless, leathery chest.

"Yes," Ikrit rasped softly. "Very interesting. I read everything I could find about this planet before we left Yavin 4. This was in the reports."

Amazed, Anakin clutched his flickering torch and watched as the leathery skin on the creature's front pulled back to reveal a patch of glowing hide, like a glowpanel in the center of its chest.

"A spotlight sloth," Ikrit murmured.

The spotlight sloth turned the light in its chest toward the colorful mushrooms. The glow grew brighter and brighter and brighter—until all of a sudden, one after another, the mushrooms began to pop. Clouds of sticky white fluff flew out in all directions. This must have been what the spotlight sloth was after, for it used its tiny paws to grab gooey tufts of spores out of the air or pluck them off its fur and stuff them into its soft, toothless mouth.

"Spotlight sloths prefer succulent flowers, but they eat other plants as well," Ikrit explained.

"That was great!" Anakin said.

"Yeah," Tahiri said, giggling.

"Wow," Uldir agreed.

Suddenly Ikrit jerked in alarm and held up a warning paw to silence the children. Immediately

Anakin could sense that the true danger was approaching. Then he saw it.

Slender jointed legs supported a plump, bulb-shaped body that was easily as large as the cargo hold in the *Lightning Rod*.

Anakin drew in a quick breath. Uldir gulped. With one finger pressed to her lips, Tahiri turned to both of them and shook her head. If Anakin hadn't been so scared, he might actually have thought it funny—Tahiri telling *him* to be quiet.

Anakin watched in horrified fascination while one of the largest spiders he had ever seen approached the entrance to their root cavern. The spider's body moved up and down as it picked its way across the muddy ground on its strong knobby legs. Anakin's heart hammered so hard against his rib cage that he almost imagined the spider could hear it. He pulled the torch as far back into the cave as he could, hoping the creature wouldn't notice them.

But the spider stopped when it reached the spotlight sloth, who was still happily munching tufts of sticky mushroom spores. So quietly that the sloth never heard it, the spider extended a stinger from its underbelly and pricked the sloth with it. A few seconds later the spotlight sloth slumped unconscious to the ground, sticky white fluff still clinging to its mouth.

Then the spider stood over the sloth and began to lower its bulbous body, bending all of its legs at once. Anakin turned his head, unable to watch. He looked at Tahiri. His friend must have been afraid she was going to scream, for she pressed both hands tightly over her mouth. Her green eyes were large and round, but she did not look away as the spider devoured its meal.

Maybe Tahiri was more used to things like this, he thought; after all, she had seen krayt dragons eat on Tatooine. But Anakin had been raised on Coruscant, a planet almost entirely covered by cities. He was *not* used to this sort of thing. Uldir had come to Yavin 4 from Coruscant, too. Anakin looked back to see how the other boy was doing.

Uldir had also turned away from the grisly scene, but when he saw Anakin watching him, he pretended to be interested in the spider's feast. It was a mistake. The moment he caught sight of the spotlight sloth—or what was left of it—Uldir gagged and retched.

Outside, the huge white spider stiffened and turned toward them. It bounced up and down on its long legs, as if it were testing their strength. It made a trumpeting sound and kicked aside the remains of the sloth. Then, with two of its powerful legs, it ripped up all of the mushrooms that grew at the base of the large tree and tossed them aside. When it finished with the mushrooms, it began uprooting smaller shrubs. The spider reached up onto the tree trunk and yanked down curtains of tough moss. Then, without warning, it began attacking the very roots of the tree under which Anakin and the others hid.

Ikrit pounded a furry fist on Artoo-Detoo's head to

get his attention. "This way—quickly!" He jumped down from the little droid and led the way.

Anakin held up his torch. Although it was a tight fit, he could see that there was just room enough for them to squeeze through the root system to emerge on the other side of the tree. Uldir needed no urging and quickly wriggled out. Artoo-Detoo scooted toward the opening, but his barrel-shaped metal body got stuck partway through.

Anakin, Tahiri, and Ikrit got behind the little droid and shoved. They had just pushed Artoo out when the tree gave an ear-shattering groan. The spider had managed to rip out enough of the roots on one side of the tree that the remaining root's tore free of the ground and the tree toppled and fell across a pool of swamp water. Anakin and Tahiri blinked as clods of dirt rained down on them and the roots of the tree, which now lay behind them, sprouted out in all directions.

Tahiri and Anakin had to push aside the muddy clumps and loose dirt that covered them to their knees before they could scoop the debris away from Artoo-Detoo and Ikrit and begin to run again. No sooner had they escaped from the tree and its roots than with a grinding, crackling sound, the spider pushed the massive trunk out of its path and followed them.

Artoo-Detoo let out an electronic wail. Anakin looked around to see where Uldir had gone but could not find him.

"Hurry," Ikrit said. "The boy is safe for now."

Tahiri yanked at Anakin's arm. "We've got to run!"

They ran. They slipped and slid over the muddy ground with the white spider in pursuit. Anakin dropped his torch and concentrated on escaping.

Ikrit ran ahead. Artoo-Detoo, who moved more slowly than the others in the mud, was soon overtaken by the spider. When Anakin and Tahiri turned to look for the droid, they saw the stinger coming down out of the white spider's underbelly. Artoo-Detoo didn't wait for it. He reached out with one of his grasper arms and clamped down hard on the stinger. At the same time, Artoo let out a high-pitched squeal that Anakin found almost deafening, even at a distance.

Suddenly, the spider seemed to think better of its attack on the little droid. It yanked in its stinger and backed up a few steps. Then, like a child throwing a tantrum, it stalked back to the uprooted tree and began ripping up all the plants in the area and flinging them aside. When it had finished that, it tore the branches off the tree as well.

Anakin and Tahiri stood still and watched in horror and fascination.

"Over here," whispered voices called. Ikrit had found Uldir. The two beckoned to them from a thick stand of trees that were much larger than any the spider had uprooted so far. Anakin and Tahiri ran to join them, followed by Artoo-Detoo, who was no longer shrieking.

"It will not harm us here," Ikrit said.

"How can you know that?" Uldir whispered.

"I have put it in the spider's mind that it is no longer hungry," Ikrit replied.

They all looked on in silence while the spider finished its "tantrum." Then it did an even more amazing thing. Climbing onto the mound of soft dirt where the old tree had been rooted, the spider settled itself, pushed its stinger down into the ground, and *planted* its legs.

Something clicked in Anakin's mind. "It's just like the tree! The trees are darker, but they have those same knobby roots."

"Yes," Ikrit said in a soft voice. "You are right . . . each of these trees was once a spider like that one over there."

Tahiri looked around at the trees. "So *these* are the grown-ups of *that*?" she said, pointing.

"Exactly, my child," Ikrit said. "There is a connection there, just as *all* things are connected through the web of energy we call the Force and through the web of life. Of course"—Ikrit's voice took on some humor now—"*some* things are more closely related than *others*."

Anakin felt something rough and scratchy against his arm. He stepped back and saw that he had been leaning against one of the tree roots. He shuddered. "I don't think I'll ever look at one of these trees in quite the same way again."

Artoo-Detoo beeped twice and then warbled.

"Our mechanical friend is right," Ikrit said. "I think he is reminding us that we should move forward again. I believe we are close to our goal."

TWELVE

"*That's* it?" Uldir asked.

They were standing outside the cave that Artoo-Detoo had led them to, and Uldir could hardly believe his eyes. There was nothing spectacular about this place. He had expected something a bit more special, unusual . . . *bigger,* at least.

The cave was beneath the spidery roots of another gigantic tree. Uldir couldn't see far into the entrance, but what he could see was ordinary enough. Moist, packed dirt, decaying leaves—nothing that would draw someone halfway across the galaxy. He could sense no special magic or power about this place.

"You're sure?" Uldir asked.

Artoo-Detoo beeped once to indicate that this was the correct cave.

Uldir snorted. "This cave doesn't look that much different from the hole under the tree where we took shelter from the rain. Just a bit deeper, that's all." He doubted that this place had any special properties. It might not even be the cave where Luke Skywalker had taken his test, he supposed. What would a little R2 unit know about such things, after all? Uldir shrugged and looked at Anakin. "You know, maybe your uncle was just in a thoughtful mood that day. I don't think he could have learned anything in this cave that he couldn't have learned if he had spent the day flying or swimming or climbing trees."

Uldir saw Anakin's forehead crinkle into a frown and he remembered what Tahiri had said about being a good friend. Maybe Anakin really was worried he had come all this way for nothing.

"Hey, I could be wrong," Uldir said. "Mind if I go in and take a look around?"

Anakin looked surprised and turned to Ikrit. "Is that okay?" he asked.

Uldir watched the furry creature nod its head.

"I think," Tahiri began uncertainly, tugging at a strand of pale yellow hair, "I think I'd like to go in, too."

Ikrit nodded his head again. "Each of you may enter," he said. "But just one at a time. Remember, the cave holds only what you take in with you."

Uldir rolled his eyes. The furry little guy was making this sound as if it was such a big deal, so meaningful. Teachers always did stuff like that, he thought—even Master Luke when he had tested Uldir for Jedi powers. Maybe it was just something Jedi teachers did to make themselves feel important. Well, he would find out soon enough, Uldir told himself.

"Okay," Uldir said, "we're agreed then. I guess I'll go first. This shouldn't take very long."

Uldir climbed down into the cave. He stood still for a moment to let his eyes adjust, but it was dark inside and Uldir couldn't see how big the cavern was. He began to walk forward.

Uldir had gotten about a meter into the cave when something touched his head and he nearly jumped out of his skin. Dirt trickled onto his hair and sifted down around him before he figured out that his head had merely brushed a low-hanging portion of the cave's roof. He stopped and pulled a glowrod out of the knapsack of provisions each of them had brought along from the ship. Turning on the glowrod, he took a look around.

The cave floor was uneven, made up mostly of rocks, roots, and dirt. Here and there piles of leaves were decaying, giving off a musty odor. The air was damp and tasted slightly spoiled. It left an oily feeling on Uldir's tongue when he opened his mouth to breathe. The cave was neither large nor small, wet nor dry. It contained nothing in any way remarkable.

Uldir gritted his teeth. He balled one hand into a fist and placed it on his hip. Maybe Master Skywalker and the furball Ikrit were just trying to convince their Jedi trainees that there was something mysterious about becoming a Jedi. Perhaps they just wanted the students to believe that there was something more to it than learning a few tricks and being taught how to be observant and how to use a lightsaber.

Well, he had seen the cave now, and it was full of nothing. Too *much* nothing. In fact, the emptiness of the cave began to press in on him. The spoiled taste and the smell of decay grew stronger. He had a strange feeling in the pit of his stomach, and he knew he had to get out of the cave right away. And after all, he asked himself, why should he stay? There was nothing more to see. . . .

Uldir turned and left the cave.

When he saw Anakin and Tahiri waiting for him, Uldir couldn't help blurting out exactly what he was thinking. "It's a hoax," he said. "That cave is empty. It's not even a very good cave."

Anakin and Tahiri looked at each other. "I think I'd like to go next if you don't mind," Tahiri said.

Uldir couldn't believe it. "Didn't you hear me?" he yelled. "There's nothing *in* there."

Artoo-Detoo gave two mournful-sounding beeps.

Ikrit, perched on the little droid's head, spoke in a sad voice. "No, you are right. For you the cave holds nothing."

Tahiri took a deep breath, trying to calm herself. No matter what Uldir said, she was certain she would see something in the cave. She didn't know what, but something, or some*one,* waited in there for her.

Tahiri pulled at a limp strand of her hair, which had become hopelessly tangled during their headlong flight from the spider. It was a mess of twigs and dirt, and still wet from the rain earlier in the afternoon, but she didn't want to waste time brushing it out now. She needed to see what was in the cave, and she knew it would be unfair to make Anakin wait any longer than he had to.

She looked at her best friend. His ice blue eyes were serious but calm, not impatient as she might have expected.

Anakin surprised her by reaching out and giving her hand a brief squeeze. "May the Force be with you," he whispered.

It was just what she'd needed. Tahiri was glad she had a good friend like Anakin. She leaned forward and whispered, "Thank you." Then she turned and went down into the cave.

The first thing Tahiri noticed was how hot the cave was. Why hadn't Uldir mentioned how *hot* it was? she wondered. Surely that was something unusual about this cave.

Scorching heat burned her nostrils as she drew hot, dry air into her lungs. A furnace blast of wind tore at her disheveled hair. It stole the moisture from her mouth, making it feel as hot and gritty as the sand beneath her feet. *Sand* . . . ?

Ghostly voices swirled around her, some speaking

the language of the Sand People from Tatooine, others speaking Basic.

Tahiri could see no sunlight or sky or even the roof of the cave, but glowing figures moved all around her. A soft glow came from the sand below, as well. The strange thing was, she could see *through* it all—the people, the sand, everything—as if she were looking at a hologram.

"Who are you?" Tahiri asked, but they didn't seem to hear or see her.

In the distance, Sand People rode banthas across the dunes. She could tell by the familiar markings on the curly-horned beasts that the tribe was her own—though from many years ago.

A few small houses with thick adobe walls appeared nearby. Humans and droids came and went from the houses, riding in speeders, trading with each other, tending to vaporators. Tahiri guessed they must be moisture farmers, as her parents had been. The humans looked almost familiar, although she couldn't be certain. Oddly enough, despite the heat and the gritty sand, one woman with long blond hair always seemed to go barefoot. The man beside her had bright green eyes. Could these have been her parents? Yes. It came to her with sudden force that they were.

Beyond the houses she saw another shadowy scene, paler this time and sparkling, as if a hologram were fading out. A scene from farther back in her own past. In this one a slender man with shoulder-length blond hair and smiling green eyes moved across a changing background, perhaps of different planets. The man must have been a Jedi, for Tahiri saw a lightsaber clipped to his belt, and she got a strange feeling that he must be related to her. Without her knowing how, the answer came to her: he was her grandfather.

Across a faint image of green grass, the man fled, pursued by Imperial stormtroopers. The man—her grandfather—turned and ran toward her. The stromtroopers shot their blaster rifles.

Though the Jedi was still far away, Tahiri reached out toward him. The stormtroopers fired their blasters again. One of the bolts flew past her grandfather and straight toward Tahiri.

A flash of blood red light burst around her, and Tahiri sank into darkness.

Then, without knowing how she had gotten there, Tahiri stood outside the cave again.

"Are you all right? What happened in there?" Anakin asked with a worried look.

"I—I'm not sure," Tahiri said. "I don't think I'm ready to talk about it yet."

She put up a hand to smooth back her tangled hair and was surprised to find that it was completely dry.

Anakin looked at Ikrit, who gave him a solemn nod. Artoo-Detoo let out a very soft warble. Uldir folded his arms across his chest and said nothing.

Tahiri placed a hand on Anakin's shoulder and whispered, "May the Force be with you, too."

Anakin hoped that he looked calm on the outside,

because on the inside he was definitely *not*. The moment he had waited for was finally here. This was why he had come to Dagobah. His quest. What if he didn't learn what he had come here to learn? What if the cave couldn't tell him whether he would fall to the dark side or become a good Jedi like Luke?

Anakin's stomach felt as if it were full of dozens of those colorful exploding mushrooms. His heart thudded painfully against his breastbone and he heard a ringing, rushing sound in his ears. But it was far too late to back out now. His mind told his feet to move and they carried him forward almost without his knowing it and then, after a short scramble down, he was in.

Inside the cave it was dim, but Anakin could see well enough. The ground was soft and slippery, like the mud outside after it rained. Here, however, unlike outside, a damp chill began to seep into his bones. Anakin shivered, wishing Tahiri had warned him so that he could have dressed more warmly. He wondered how long he would have to wait before the cave showed him what was in his mind. Uldir and Tahiri had each been gone only a few minutes. Why hadn't anything happened yet?

Anakin drew in a slow, calming breath. To his relief, he felt warm air flow into his lungs. Warm, clear light like a summer sunrise dawned on one side of him.

On the other side, the cave seemed to grow darker still. Lightning flashed across the darkened half of the cave, and a frigid rain began to fall.

Anakin raised both hands in front of his face. One was wet, the other dry. One cold, one warm. What was happening?

The next flash of lightning revealed a figure wearing a flowing black cape and a glossy black plasteel helmet.

Anakin's back and shoulders went rigid. The breath froze in his lungs. He opened his mouth to cry out, but before he could, a second figure appeared—this one in the bright, sunlit part of the cave.

The new figure wore a brown hooded robe, and his bearded face was mostly hidden. A lightsaber hung from a belt tied around his robe.

Bolts of blue lightning crackled through the cave, but this time they did not come from the storm. The figure on the darkened side of the cave held his hands out, fingers spread. The blue lightning arched from his fingertips toward the Light Jedi, who shielded himself from the attack, although he did not hurl any blue fire toward the dark side of the cave.

Anakin's legs were trembling with tension. He found his breathing coming in gasps. Blue fire crackled out again, this time followed by cruel laughter. Anakin knew he had to do something. He snapped out of his stupor and threw himself between the light and the darkness.

"No," he said. "I won't let you!"

Dark lightning danced and crackled toward him and he threw up an arm to ward it off.

"I said *no*!" he yelled.

The two figures stopped and turned their faces toward him. A bright haze swam before Anakin's eyes.

Both of the faces were his.

THIRTEEN

Anakin and Tahiri huddled close together around a small cook fire that Ikrit had built. Uldir sat across the fire from them, a sour expression on his face, his arms once more folded across his chest. Anakin guessed that the older boy hadn't believed a word that he or Tahiri said, but that didn't really matter to Anakin. Right now, all he cared about was getting some answers.

Anakin looked at Ikrit. "So what did it all mean?"

Tahiri looked to Ikrit as well. Except for when she told her story in a slow, halting voice, she had not spoken at all since coming out of the cave.

"As different as you are from one another, my young students," Ikrit rasped, "the things you each saw in the cave are not as unlike as you might believe. And for each of you, the lesson is much the same. Your learning and heritage mold you. No one is either entirely good or bad. Your parents, your experiences, your past and your present all combine to make you the person that you are.

"We each contain the potential for great good or great evil. We each hold the shadow of darkness . . . and the flame of light. Our destinies are not set, and life offers no guarantees. It is the choices that you make . . . that will determine what you become."

Ikrit looked at Tahiri. "It is not who raised us or who our parents were that determines our paths."

Now Ikrit turned his solemn blue-green eyes toward Anakin. "The Emperor cannot reach out to you from beyond the grave—but neither can those you love make your choices for you. You will become what you become because of *your* choices . . . because of what *you* do."

Uldir snorted impolitely. "*I* could have told you that. I choose to be a Jedi. You make your choice, and that's all there is to it."

Tahiri ignored the sour remark. Her bright green eyes searched Anakin's face. "Is that what you needed to learn? Did you find what you were looking for?"

Anakin closed his eyes and searched deep inside himself. The urgent need to know what he would become was no longer there. He still wasn't sure what his future would be; no one could be. But he knew that he would have to trust the Force and make his choices carefully. And he suddenly realized that he was no longer afraid.

Anakin opened his eyes and smiled at his best friend. "It wasn't at all what I expected," he said. "But I found the answer I needed. I guess we can all go back to Yavin 4 now and—"

"No. Not yet," the voice of Ikrit broke in. "We have one last stop to make before my own quest here is fulfilled."

Tahiri and Anakin exchanged surprised glances.

Anakin had thought he was the only one in the group with a reason for coming to Dagobah. In his urgent need to find answers, had he missed something?

"Where are we going, Ikrit?"

The white-furred Jedi Master bounded to the top of Artoo-Detoo's domed head. "Put out the fire," he said gruffly, as if it was difficult for him to speak right now. "The droid will show us the way."

Artoo-Detoo gave a triumphant warble.

"I guess that means we're here," Anakin said.

The companions stood around a small but well-built structure that must once have been a house. The outside was not destroyed in any way, but it looked as if no one had lived inside for a long time. Through the window Anakin could see that rodents, snakes, and flying creatures had made their nests among the moss and cobwebs that now covered all of the furniture.

Tahiri peered inside. "It must have been very cozy once," she said.

"It's pretty small, though" Uldir observed.

"Size matters not," Ikrit replied.

"Well, it sure doesn't *look* like much," Uldir said, his voice changing and cracking as he spoke. "Why would you want to visit this?"

Anakin cringed at Uldir's rude words. Ikrit seemed to take no offense.

"This was the home of Yoda," Ikrit said. "A great Jedi Master." He leapt from Artoo's head through the open window and sat on the leaf-littered stone floor. For minutes he sat there studying the tiny dwelling.

Under the mud and dirt that Ikrit had picked up during their adventures, it seemed to Anakin that the Jedi Master's white fur had turned an unhealthy shade of gray. "Are you all right?" he asked.

"Yoda was . . . a noble Jedi," Ikrit replied slowly. "He served the Old Republic for hundreds of years. He taught many students and fought against evil wherever he found it. But in the end, he was forced into hiding here to escape the Emperor's slaughter of the Jedi."

By the time the Jedi Master finished speaking, his beautiful white coat had turned entirely black.

Tahiri gasped. "Master Ikrit, your fur!"

"I didn't know that you could do that," Anakin said in amazement. "Change colors, I mean."

"There is much you do not know about me," the Jedi Master rasped. "My people have long had the ability to change colors, to camouflage themselves for safety . . . or to mourn. I mourn Yoda, a great Jedi Master."

"How do you know so much about Yoda?" asked Anakin.

"It was he who found me on Kushibah," Ikrit said, "chose me and trained me, just as he trained your uncle. Yoda was *my* Jedi Master, too."

While Anakin and Tahiri watched openmouthed with astonishment, Master Ikrit shook himself and flung away all traces of mud and dirt from his silky coat.

Then his fur blossomed again to a snowy white.

Anakin wondered how many more surprises and secrets Ikrit had in store for them.

FOURTEEN

Tahiri couldn't help giggling at the look on old Peckhum's face.

"I don't know how I'm supposed to squeeze in one more passenger on the way back to Yavin 4," the grizzled spacer exclaimed. "Maybe I should just let Uldir ride back in the hold—didn't seem to bother him when he stowed away the first time, since he went ahead and did it again."

Peckhum grumbled for a while, then agreed to make room for Uldir. It took some creative thinking and hours of rearranging in the cockpit, but they managed it in the end.

Tahiri plunked herself into her seat and immediately removed her boots with a happy groan. She wiggled her toes. There was still a bandage wrapped around the cut on her right foot. Even so, she felt freer and more comfortable right away. "That's better," she said to no one in particular. She sat back in her seat and buckled her crash webbing.

With Anakin's and Uldir's seats wedged in next to Tahiri's, the cockpit was crowded, but that couldn't be helped. Ikrit, the last one in, climbed back onto Anakin's shoulder and strapped himself in place.

Tahiri flexed her bare toes again. "I was lucky my feet didn't get hurt a lot worse," she said. She tugged at a strand of her pale yellow hair. "I'll have to remember to thank Tionne for thinking to send those boots for me."

And she did.

With a smile, Anakin watched Uldir slosh another bucketful of river water onto the deckplates in the hold of the *Lightning Rod*. Tahiri squealed and giggled as the warm river water ran across her bare feet.

Anakin and Uldir both chuckled as well. Uldir went for more water, and Anakin picked up the scrub brush again.

The return trip from Dagobah had gone smoothly. When they got back to Yavin 4, Artoo-Detoo had warbled happily to be reunited with his master, and Luke had looked both happy and relieved. Tionne had given each of the travelers, including Uldir, a big hug.

Anakin, Tahiri, and Uldir each had a long private meeting with Luke and then with Tionne. In fact, there was so much talking and meeting and hugging that at the end of a few hours, Anakin was convinced that there was no one left who hadn't already talked to everyone else. But he was wrong.

Anakin was still in his uncle's office when Ikrit showed up on the Jedi Master's windowsill. Anakin felt more at peace now than he had in months, so he didn't mind at all when Luke asked him to go with Tahiri and Uldir to clean the mud out of the *Lightning Rod*'s cockpit and hold. The two Jedi Masters needed some time alone to talk.

The assignment seemed only fair to Anakin. After all, old Peckhum had gone pretty far out of his way to take him to Dagobah on his quest. And Peckhum would need the swamp mud out of his hold before he could haul any more supplies.

And so Anakin and Tahiri had worked willingly and happily for the rest of the day. Uldir had been a bit more reserved, but warmed up as they worked and joked together.

Uldir returned, dumped his bucket of water on the deckplates, plopped down on his knees in the puddle, and began scrubbing. He sighed. "Do you think I'll ever become a Jedi?" he asked.

There was a brief, uncomfortable silence.

"Maybe," Tahiri said. "I don't really know enough about how it works."

Anakin shrugged. "It's possible," he said. "Even Jedi Masters can make mistakes. Uncle Luke told me that when he left Dagobah the first time, Yoda thought Uncle Luke would never become a Jedi. But he did."

Tahiri sat back on her heels and tossed her blond

hair out of her face. "Whether you become a Jedi or not, Uldir, if that's what you want, we'll help as much as we can."

Anakin nodded his agreement.

Uldir smiled. "Thanks, both of you. I'll go get us some more water."

Uldir trudged down to the river with an empty bucket and a heart full of stubborn determination.

He *would* become a Jedi. He would show them that he could do it.

Uldir was sure that if he just had the right equipment—a lightsaber, Jedi robes—and the same training and opportunities as Anakin and Tahiri, he would become a Jedi.

He decided that he would start wearing the robes of a Jedi right away, with a belt that could hold his lightsaber when he got far enough along in his training. Then everyone would see that he was serious.

Yes, he decided. He would show them all.

"There, that's better," Tahiri said, surveying their handiwork.

Anakin dried the last puddle of water off the deckplates by the ramp. The hold of the *Lightning Rod* sparkled and gleamed, as clean as they had ever seen it.

"Anyone up there?" a voice called through the hatch.

"Uncle Luke!" Anakin said.

Master Luke Skywalker walked up the ramp, with Tionne and Master Ikrit beside him. Artoo-Detoo scooted up the ramp after them.

"You kids seem to be doing pretty well on your assignment," Tionne said.

Anakin spread his arms as if to show off their handiwork. "All finished," he said. "Our mission is a success."

"We all learned a lot on Dagobah," Tahiri added. "But I'm glad the adventure is over now."

Luke, Tionne, and Ikrit looked at each other. Luke chuckled. He put one hand on Anakin's shoulder and one on Tahiri's. "Somehow," he said, "knowing you two, I think you will have plenty more adventures to come."

Behind him Artoo-Detoo gave a loud beep of agreement.

STAR WARS®

Junior Jedi Knights

VADER'S FORTRESS

Anakin has been having terrible dreams of a secret cave on Dagobah. He asks his uncle Luke if he can go there, to see if it's real. Luke says yes—but only if Tahiri, R2-D2, and the Jedi Master Ikrit go along.

Anakin and his friends find more danger than they bargained for in the swamps of Dagobah. But they do find the cave. What is inside? And will Anakin be strong enough in the Force to face it?

Turn the page for a special preview
of the next book in the
STAR WARS: JUNIOR JEDI KNIGHTS series:
VADER'S FORTRESS
Coming in July from Boulevard Books!

Drops of moisture sparkled on the short grass of the landing field in front of the Jedi academy. The sunlight on Yavin 4 seemed especially bright after the morning's rain. Smells of leaves and flowers drifted from the jungle nearby. The air felt comfortably damp and warm to Anakin Solo, who gazed expectantly toward the sky. He brushed his fringe of straight brown bangs away from his ice blue eyes and then shaded them with one hand so that he could see better.

The ship should arrive soon, he thought.

Anakin's best friend Tahiri stood beside him, barefoot in the grassy stubble. Her pale yellow hair blew free in the breeze, and her sea green eyes also looked skyward. Beside her waited Uldir, the strong teenage son of two cargo pilots. Shaggy chestnut hair framed his proud face. Uldir had stowed away and come to the Jedi academy in hopes of becoming a Jedi. He had persuaded Anakin's uncle, Luke Skywalker, to accept him as a Jedi trainee for a while, even though the teen had no real talent with the Force. Although Uldir was several years older than Anakin, the two youngest Jedi trainees had befriended the new student.

Both Tahiri and Uldir were unusually silent today, and Anakin felt himself growing impatient. "We've been waiting almost an hour," Anakin said. "Do you think something's wrong?"

Uldir shrugged. Tahiri didn't respond. Anakin shifted his weight. So far, he had managed to amuse himself by solving puzzles in his head, but he was getting tired of standing. He wanted to sit down, but he knew the wet grass would soak his comfortable flightsuit in no time. He wasn't sure that would feel any better than just standing.

Even though Tahiri was a couple of years younger than he was, the long wait this morning didn't seem to bother her at all. Uldir whistled a tune under his breath and retied the belt of his new brown Jedi robe. Anakin guessed it made Uldir feel more like a student to have a robe like the ones Jedi Masters often wore.

A Jedi needs to be patient, Anakin reminded himself. Taking a deep breath, he did one of his calming exercises using the Force. He thought back on the quest that had recently taken them all to the planet Dagobah. He, Tahiri, and Uldir had had many adventures there, guided by the Jedi Master Ikrit. One at a time, the three junior Jedi had gone into a special cave to find out about who they were inside. In the cave Anakin and Tahiri had learned that their parents and the people in their past were a part of who each of them were today. But now they also knew that only their *own* choices could decide who they would become. Uldir had seen nothing in the cave, though, and Anakin wondered if the older boy had learned anything.

"I don't think so," Tahiri said suddenly. Just like that, with no explanation.

"Huh?" Anakin blinked at her. "*What* don't you think?"

Tahiri shrugged. "I don't think that there's anything wrong, of course. That *is* what you asked, isn't it? You asked if I thought that anything was wrong. And I don't. So I said—"

"Yes . . . yes, I heard you," Anakin said. "I only meant—"

Tahiri gave him an odd look. "Really, Anakin! Sometimes I wonder how you manage to get so confused even during a simple conversation. And anyway, I don't know why you'd think that anything might be wrong. Master Skywalker wouldn't have sent us out here to meet Tionne if he hadn't been sure she was going to get here sooner or later. So I'm positive that everything is fine. Relax and enjoy the beautiful weather. She'll be here any time now."

"Well, I hope she hurries," Uldir said. His amber eyes searched the sky. "I don't have much time before my next shift working in the kitchen. I thought we were going to go into the jungle together so you could give me some tips on using the Force to lift leaves."

"We'll have plenty of time to practice," Tahiri said confidently.

"I just wish there was an easier way to learn about the Force," Uldir said. His voice had started low, but changed with a squeak in midsentence. "It always seems like such hard work."

"I guess I don't think about whether it's hard to study the Force and practice, because I enjoy it so much," Anakin admitted.

Tahiri gave Uldir an encouraging smile. "I have a feeling you're going to start catching on pretty soon now. After all, when Tionne found me on Tatooine—"

"That's Uncle Luke's homeworld, you know," Anakin explained to Uldir.

"Right," Tahiri said. "Anyway, when Tionne found me out in the middle of the desert living with the Sand People, I didn't know any more about using the Force than you—but look how much I've learned already. Tionne is a natural teacher, and I'm never bored when she's talking. That's why I love to go along on her research trips, you know. I wish I could have gone with her this time to Borgo Prime. . . . I always learn so much." Tahiri looked pensive for a moment; then her face brightened. "Well, she did promise to take me with her on her next research trip. Traveling with her is always an adventure. I hope—"

"That sounds fun," Anakin said. "I wonder if she'd mind if I came along with you."

"Yeah, me too," Uldir said.

"Well, you can ask her yourself," Tahiri said, pointing upward. "That must be her now. But where did she get that strange ship? I've never seen it before."

A ship had indeed arrived and was floating down through the air toward the landing field. The craft was very old and had a strange design, with a plump reddish-orange body and broad solar sails that collected sunlight to power the ship. The shimmering metallic sails spread out on each side like wings, making the craft look something like a pudgy copper dragon.

Tahiri seemed to dance with excitement as they waited for the ship to land. When the orange sails finally folded and the spacecraft touched down, Tahiri could contain herself no longer. She ran forward, shouting a greeting as her good friend and Jedi instructor Tionne stepped down from the odd little ship.

Anakin wanted to give the two of them a chance to talk before he joined them, so he hung back for a moment with Uldir. He could sense through the Force that Tionne was just as giddy as the blonde-haired girl, but he couldn't tell what the excitement was about.

Watching the talkative girl and the quiet Jedi

instructor together always made Anakin smile. In spite of their differences, the two shared a close bond. They could almost be mother and daughter, Anakin mused. Since Tahiri's mother had died when she was only three, he wondered if she did think of the Jedi teacher that way.

Beside Anakin, Uldir cleared his throat impatiently and fidgeted with his robe. "Okay," Anakin said, "I guess we can go help Tionne now." They started forward.

"Welcome back," Anakin called.

"Hi," Uldir said.

Tionne turned. Her large mother-of-pearl eyes sparkled with delight at seeing them. "It's good to be back," she said. "Even better because I have such exciting news for Master Skywalker."

"So you found something?" Anakin asked.

Tionne smiled in an I've-got-a-secret kind of way. "Quite a bit, actually. But first, what do you think of my new ship?"

Uldir snorted. "If that's a *new* model, then I'm the son of a nerf herder."

The silvery-haired instructor gave a musical laugh. "You're right, of course. The *Lore Seeker*—that's what I named my ship—is really quite old. That's why I loved the design so much."

"Well, I think the ship is perfect for you," Tahiri said. "It's just right. And so is the name."

Anakin nodded. He knew Tionne had called her craft the *Lore Seeker* because she loved to look for stories and legends about Jedi who lived long ago. He closed his eyes for a moment and reached into the ship with his mind. "It's in excellent condition," he announced, and looked up at Tionne with surprise.

"I'm glad to hear you say that," the Jedi instructor said with a smile. "I thought so, too. But because the ship was so old, I was able to buy it from a Randoni trader for a song."

"How much did you *really* pay?" Uldir asked.

Tionne shrugged. "Just a song. Really. While I was looking for Jedi legends, I came across an ancient song that told about the very first Randoni merchants and the vaults where they hid their wealth. The trader was so interested that she offered me the *Lore Seeker* in exchange for the song. Now come help me unload my cargo and I'll show you some of my other treasures."

Anakin and Tahiri needed no more urging. They hurried to explore the strange ship and help Tionne. Uldir grumbled something about never getting the fun jobs, but he went along with them anyway.

Inside the *Lore Seeker*'s tiny hold, Tionne said, "You may carry this Twi'lek story-chain, Tahiri—each link tells a different part of a story. Please be very careful with it. Uldir, here is a holodisk. It holds a recording of some very old Jedi songs. Anakin, would you please carry this scroll? I'll take the tapestry."

On the way back to the Jedi academy they each

carried their packages with extra care. As usual, Tahiri chattered gaily. "I can't wait to see Master Skywalker's face when you show him everything you found. He'll probably want to see the *Lore Seeker* right away. Have you learned any of the old songs from that holodisk yet? Will you sing them to us?"

"You sure seem to have had a successful trip," Anakin put in.

Tionne tossed back her silvery hair and chuckled. "Oh, that's not all—I found something even more important. I learned where to find an object that may have more meaning for Master Skywalker than any of these treasures we're holding."

"Well, where is it then?" Tahiri said.

"In an old fortress on a planet called Vjun," Tionne said.

"Does anyone live in the fortress?" Anakin asked.

Tionne shook her head. "Not anymore."

"Well, if it's really that important, don't you think you ought to go find it?" Tahiri said. "And don't forget that you promised to take me with you this time."

"I'd like to go along, too," Anakin added.

"Yeah, it sounds like fun," Uldir said.

Tionne frowned. "I'm not sure Master Skywalker will approve. It could be a bit dangerous. The news about this special thing had just reached Borgo Prime, but there might be other people who learned about where it is—other people who might want to find it too."

"Then it sounds important enough that we ought to go after it," Tahiri insisted. "As soon as possible."

"Why would someone else want it?" Anakin asked, his ice blue eyes alive with curiosity. "What kind of special object is this?"

Tionne's face lit with a wondering smile, and she gave a happy sigh. "It's Obi-Wan Kenobi's lightsaber!"

About the Author

Rebecca Moesta Anderson knew she wanted to be an author since her early teens, but it wasn't until six years ago that she began writing in earnest. Rebecca has worked on numerous *Star Wars* projects. With her husband, Kevin J. Anderson, she created and wrote the young adult novels in the Young Jedi Knights series and two high-tech pop-up books. She has also authored several science fiction stories (both on her own and with her husband) and has cowritten three science fiction and fantasy novels under a pseudonym.

Born in Heidelberg, Germany, to American parents, Rebecca was raised in Pasadena, California. After receiving a Masters of Science degree in Business Administration from Boston University, she worked for more than seven years as a technical editor and writer at Lawrence Livermore National Laboratory, a large government research facility in California.

Rebecca Moesta has one son, who keeps her busy nearly every minute that she doesn't spend writing.

Rebecca Moesta and Kevin J. Anderson's
WordFire website may be reached at
http://www.wordfire.com

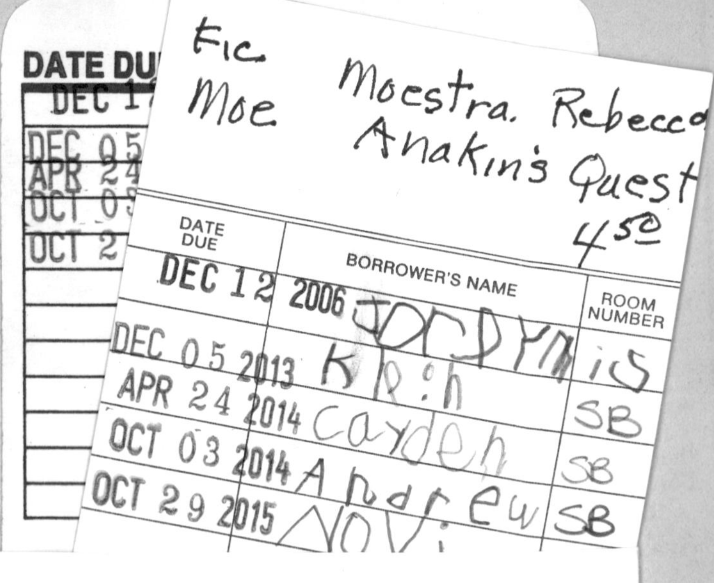

DATE DU

DEC 1

DEC 05

APR 24

OCT 0

OCT 2

Fic
Moe

Moestra. Rebecca
Anakin's Quest

4 50

DATE DUE	BORROWER'S NAME	ROOM NUMBER
DEC 12 2006	JORDYN	
DEC 05 2013	Krih	iS
APR 24 2014	cayden	SB
OCT 03 2014	Andrew	SB
OCT 29 2015	NOVi	SB